Great Stories
of the
Great Plains

Tales of the Dakotas - Volume 2

By
Keith Norman

GREAT STORIES OF THE GREAT PLAINS
TALES OF THE DAKOTAS - VOLUME 2

Copyright © 2004 by Keith Norman

All rights reserved.

No part of this book may be reproduced or transmitted in any form or by any means electronic or mechanical, including photocopying, recording, or by any information storage and retrieval system, without permission in writing from the copyright owner.

Author - Keith Norman
Publisher - McCleery & Sons Publishing

International Standard Book Number: 1-931916-39-X
Printed in the United States of America

This Book is dedicated to
My Father
Thomas Norman

For His Friendship and
The Example of his Life

And, as Always to
My Wife
Calamity Jane
Whose Not Nearly as Young as She Used to Be,
Nor Nearly as Old as I Plan for Her to Grow
Beside Me.

Preface

George Santayana, a Spanish born philosopher who lived much of his life in the United States, wrote 'Those who cannot learn from history are doomed to repeat it'. Certainly in the history of the Dakotas there are many incidents that we hope we have learned enough from to never see again.

The clashes of cultures that resulted in massacres at places like the Little Bighorn River and Wounded Knee Creek come to mind. Or the epidemics of dreaded diseases like small pox that took the lives of the majority of the Native American population in 1837, and influenza that claimed 5% of the population regardless of race 81 years later. Or the winter of 1880 when the blizzards started in mid October and continued to assault the population of the region, most of which were living in tar paper shacks, until April.

The list of disasters, diseases and historic blunders that we hope and pray to never see again could be almost endless. But the inventory of this region's historic wonders, events that many people, myself included, would love to be able to relive, is equally lengthy.

Many of us would love to be with Captains Lewis and Clark as they explore the prairies and mountains unseen by white men's eyes, or along with General Custer as he and the 7th Cavalry toured the Black Hills. Or maybe a chance to relive the less epic episodes of Dakota history appeals to you. Things like riding the range with Ed Lemmon in the biggest pasture in the world, or spending Saturday night in a railhead cow town partying with the cowboys. Possibly making a little moonshine in a hidden still during the days of prohibition would make your day.

When I research these stories I often ask myself how I would have reacted in the situation. I try to relive, at least in my mind, the little piece of history I'm writing about. My hope is that I convey to you, the reader, the same opportunity, the chance to relive the past if only in your imagination, in each of these tales.

Again, there are so many people to thank for the support and help that they give me in these projects. Thanks to my proofreaders, Thomas

Norman, my father and my mother-in-law Beverly Ecker. They make what is quite often a mishmash of thoughts a readable story. Thanks to the people at McCleery and Sons who make publishing a book a painless process. Thanks to Agnes and the ladies at the Stutsman County Library who never cease to amaze me with the books they find for me. And a special thanks to my wife, Jane, who believes in my small gifts and abilities but still has the courage to question the more than occasional really bad idea.

But the biggest thanks go to the people who listen to our radio shows and have bought our books. Their support, not only in the form of purchases but their comments and listenership has made this endeavor a joy to pursue.

Table of Contents

An English Cattle Drive 1
The Time of the Ferries 2
Minimum Work for Minimum Wage 3
Rain Along the River 4
Row, Row, Row Your Boat 5
Two Ladies Go For a Ride 6
A Whale of a Time 7
Wrong Side Up 8
Cards, Guns, and Petticoats 9
Pomp and Circumstance 10
Fool Soldiers to the Rescue 11
The City of Swans.. 12
The White River Cure 13
A Really Shortline 14
But Captain What Will We Put on the Toast?.............. 15
Love, Murder and Horses 16
Park It Over There 17
Man the Lifeboats 18
Death and Taxes 19
We're Looking for Mr. D. Boone 20
Marching on Their Stomachs 21
Head'em Up, and Move'em Out 22
One Ringee Dingee.. 23
The Journey Begins.. 24
Self Defense on the Back Roads 25
Let it Burn 26
The Indians Aren't Coming.. 27
Which Rock Should It Be? 28
Let's Get This Expedition on the Road.......................... 29
A Bridge Over Muddy Waters 30
If We Can't Invade Canada, Let's Go West 31
Mister Chairman 32
A Five Hundred Century Old Park 33
Giving Peace a Chance 34
An Artist in all Mediums... 35
The Cow Jumped Over the Moon 36

Now We're in a Pickle 37

The Plague of 1918 38

No Water in the Well, But Gold? 40

Oh, Say Can You See 41

Medora Returns to Medora 42

It's Dark Down in This Basement 43

Riding the Line 44

Take Two Mad Dog Plants and Call Me in the Morning 45

The State of Lincoln 46

The One-Sided Shootout at LeBeau 47

The Fighting Irishman from South Dakota 48

The Atomic Bomb from Canton 49

A Guide and a Mom 50

Fannie and Nellie on the James 51

Governor Bigelow of Vermillion 52

A Gold Mine for the South Dakota Treasury 53

She Got the House in the Settlement 54

A Lady Doctor and Her Family 55

The Wizard of South Dakota 56

Put Another Cow Chip on the Fire 57

Herding on the Cheyenne Strip 58

Take a Left at Washington 59

The Big Bang Theory 60

He Couldn't Take Home a Souvenir Spoon 61

Uff-da, I Have to Go to School 62

The Devil's Dictionary 63

Motor Cars and Laws 64

Free Speech on the Prairie 65

Grigsby's Roughriders 67

A Walking Stick by Any Other Name 68

Camel Feed for the Dakotas 69

The Blood Thirsty Hoards of Fort Union 70

The Elk's Suspenders 71

Vote Early, Vote Often 72

Let's Build Us a New Elevator 73

A Colorful Foreigner 74

Crawling the Walls at Fort Mandan 75

Let's Count the Cash 76

The South Dakota Courtesy Patrol 77

Death of a Legend 78
By God, We Need a Motto 79
Give Me a Beer 80
Charging for Cheap Land 81
Stagecoaches, Fires and Curses 82
A Rock by Any Other Name 83
Up, Up and Away 84
The Gang that Couldn't Ride Straight 85
I'm the Governor, But of What? 86
Early Team Sports on the Prairie 87
They Hang Horse Thieves 88
The 'South Dakota Today' 89
A Steam Belching, Water Walking, Dragon 90
The 'W Bar' Spread 91
Where'd That Horse Wander Off To? 92
An Underground Marriage 93
Doughboys, Doctors and Nurses 94
Wages and Retirement 95
Take Ten Paces and Check Your Shirt 96
A Quick Game of Billiards 97
Chalk One Up for the Indians 98
Let's Have the Neighbors Over 99
Hook Mama to the Travois 100
Tote That Bag 101
A Horse, of Course 102
We're Out Here for the Hats 103
A Massacre in the Snow 104
Hot Time in the Old Town 105
A Little Cabin at the World's Fair 106
Where Do You Want Me to Park the House? 108
Army Discipline Vs. Tribal Discipline 109
Hauling a Heavy Load 110
Champagne for Everyone 111
And They're Off 112
Ride'em Hollywood Cowboy 113
A Native Frontier Army 114
Dead Bill in Deadwood 115
The Yellowstone Expedition of 1873 116
Sending Out For Buffalo 118

A Prairie Temper Tantrum 119
Old Enemies on the Prairie 120
Custer's Gold 122
Wild Times in Dickinson 123
There's Gold in Them Thar Cats 124
Look at Them Legs 125
Set Em' Up Doc 126
A Maid Today, Bride Tomorrow 127
The Little Phone Exchange on the Prairie 128
Flying North 129
Rumors of Our Death are Greatly Exaggerated 131
The Ancient and Honorable Profession of Horse Stealing 132
An Officer and a Gentleman 133

An English Cattle Drive

Moreton Frewen was an English remittance man, a group of people from good European families that were often given an allowance and told to live away from their home country. While Frewen roamed the world with a number of business schemes he made a major investment in the American West in the late 1870's.

Frewen built a ranch near Cheyenne, Wyoming and started raising cattle. When you raise cattle you need to sell them. His plan was to drive the cattle across the Dakotas and Minnesota to Duluth. Load them on Great Lakes ships for transportation east to the St. Lawrence River which was not navigatable by ships at that time; transfer them to trains for shipping to the Atlantic Coast. They could then be loaded on Ocean Liners and shipped to England.

Obviously such a journey would leave the cattle a little thin so Frewen planned to feed his livestock in England before sending them off to slaughter. Unfortunately, English law mandated that imported cattle be slaughtered immediately to prevent the spreading of foreign diseases.

Frewen made numerous trips to England to recruit investors for his Powder River Livestock Company and to lobby to change the laws regarding the slaughter of imported cattle. Ultimately the law doesn't change and the ranch goes bankrupt. Just one of many business failures around the world that Moreton Frewen will promote that loses investor's fortunes.

Despite his lack of successes in business Moreton is well connected politically and socially. He was welcomed at the White House to confer with Presidents for decades. His friendships within the literary world included Oscar Wilde and Rudyard Kipling. American author Owen Wister drew some of the scenes for his book 'The Virginian' from Frewen's experience on the Wyoming frontier.

Through all of these businesses and moves around the world Moreton's wife kept in touch with her sister, the wife of Lord Randall Churchill, and the mother of Winston Churchill.

The Time of the Ferries

As railroads built more and more branch lines around the Dakotas the role of the steamboat on the Missouri River changed. It was no longer needed to move goods up and down the river from railhead ports such as Yankton or Bismarck. But until bridges became common across the Big Muddy riverboats still were important.

While pontoon bridges were used in some locations, quite often it was the riverboat that moved people and goods from one side of the river to the other. Often it was cattle that were ferried across from the big rangelands west of the Missouri to the railheads on the east.

Captain Senechal was one of the last of the Missouri riverboat pilots. During his lengthy career in the ferry boat business he never lost a cow. If any cattle jumped over the side they were roped and dragged along side the boat to the other side.

The same could not be said for a crate of chickens that fell off a wagon that was being loaded on board. When they last were seen Captain Senechal said they were 'headed for the Gulf'.

Senechal tried a number of enterprises along the river. He and his sons ran excursion boats to the buffalo pastures west of Pierre and even put together a floating Wild West Show that toured the southern Missouri ports.

But in the end it was progress that ended the days of the ferry boat. Captain Senechal retired to a home in Phillip, South Dakota in the mid 1920's, right after the fifth bridge crossed the Missouri in the Dakotas.

Minimum Work for Minimum Wage

The federal government first instituted a minimum wage in 1938. The base salary for Americans was set at 25 cents per hour but only applied to workers involved in interstate trade or producing goods for interstate trade. This amounts to a wage of a little over $3.00 per hour in current dollars. One year later the minimum wage was raised to 30 cents per hour.

But in this issue the state of South Dakota was way ahead of Washington. South Dakota had established a minimum wage law in 1923. The Industrial Commissioner was in charge of enforcement. Not only could underpaid workers sue their employer for the wages they were shorted but criminal charges could be filed. Bosses that underpaid their employees could be fined up to $100 and be sentenced to up to 30 days in jail.

But what was the bottom line for a working man's wage in South Dakota in 1923? The law set the minimum wage at $12 per week which would amount to 30 cents per hour based on a 40 hour work week. My guess is that South Dakota used a weekly rate rather than an hourly rate in deference to the long hours worked in agriculture.

However, there were a couple of exceptions to the law. Apprentices could be paid less than the base allowed by law during their training. And women over the age of 14, 'physically or mentally deficient' could receive a special permit to work for less than minimum wage. There was no allowance for disabled men to work for less.

Rain Along the River

By the 1840's there was concern among the few American citizens in the Red River Valley that Canadians were crossing the border and illegally trading with the Indians. Add to this the complaint by Father Belcourt to the United States Indian Commissioner that northern hunters were taking buffalo south of the border leaving poor hunting for the Indians.

The argument was made that since the Hudson Bay Company had established its own post of Fort Garry near present day Winnipeg the Americans should have a fort of their own along the border.

The army responded by sending an expedition into the region. On June 6, 1849 Major Samuel Woods left Fort Snelling marching west. They crossed the Red near present day Wahpeton, North Dakota and established a temporary post on the sight where Fort Abercrombie would later be built before heading north along the river.

That summer of 1849 was wetter than normal. Mosquitoes swarmed making life miserable for man and beast. Most of the rivers were flooded and difficult to cross. When the expedition reached Pembina and wanted to return east to the Mississippi they were delayed for a month by the twenty foot high Red River.

But it was during this wait that Major Woods learned about the agricultural bounty of the basin. The Selkirk colonist near Pembina told him of 40 bushel per acre wheat, 50 bushels of oats or barley, and up to 300 bushels an acre of potatoes.

During their travels the expedition meets with both the Métis and the Indians of the region. The Métis were in favor of opening the region to white settlement while the Native Americans were said to listen to the talk of settlement in 'grim silence'.

Major Woods and his party did not build a fort along the Red. In fact no real settlement occurs in the area for nearly another quarter century. This despite the glowing reports of the rich farm lands of the Red River Valley.

Row, Row, Row Your Boat

John Jacob Astor was already the undisputed king of the fur trade. With the return of the Lewis and Clark expedition he saw an opportunity to expand his empire.

His plan was to establish a trading post along the Pacific Coast near the mouth of the Columbia River. He sent one group of traders by sea, around South America, to Oregon. To hedge his bet another group was sent overland, along the Missouri River, to the same destination.

Astor's expedition was headed by Walter Hunt. When he arrived in St. Louis in the fall of 1810 he soon realized that Manuel Lisa was also planning on making a trip up the Missouri the next spring. Instead of pooling their resources it became a rivalry for fur trade superiority.

Hunt and the Astor crew got the jump on Lisa by moving their winter camp 400 miles upstream that fall. Even with that head start it was a neck and neck race up the Missouri between the Lisa and Astor boats during the spring of 1811.

Both crews were concerned that whoever reached the Sioux on the plains of the Dakotas first would incite the Indians against the other. They needn't have been worried. When the two parties did meet in June near present day Pierre, South Dakota it became obvious that the Astor party was planning on continuing to the Pacific Ocean while Lisa traded with the Arikara and then returned to St. Louis.

When Hunt continued on his way to the Pacific Coast he took a different route than the previous Lewis and Clark expedition. His expedition left the Missouri and traveled west along the Grand River. They became the first white travelers to the cross the northern Black Hills before continuing on through the Rockies on their way to the Columbia River.

Manuel Lisa became one of the major fur traders of the Missouri River Basin. The enterprises of John Jacob Astor dominated the fur trade in the Rocky Mountains and Pacific Northwest.

Two Ladies Go For a Ride

On May 17, 1876 the parade ground at Fort Abraham Lincoln was crowded. Nearly 900 men and a like number of horses and mules were set to pass inspection and start their march west. Despite the foggy and misty weather we can assume that the porches of the officer's quarters were lined by misty eyed wives and sweethearts as well.

But a couple of those wives weren't on the porches but instead were riding alongside their husbands. Libbie Custer and Maggie Calhoun accompanied the 7th on its first day of march. Maggie was General Custer's sister and was married to James Calhoun. Jimmie had been an infantry officer when he had met Maggie six years earlier. When they married Custer had him transferred to the cavalry and added a brother-in-law to the royal family of the 7th. He often served as Custer's adjutant.

The two ladies accompanied their husbands to the first night's camp along the Heart River. Libbie and Maggie returned to Fort Lincoln with the regimental paymaster the next day. It was the last time they would see their husbands.

Less than six weeks later these women were widows; their officer husbands were killed on the hills above the Little Bighorn River in Montana. They learned the fate of their mates when the Far West brought the wounded from Reno's command back to Fort Lincoln late on the evening of July 5th.

A Whale of a Time

The two winters that the members of the Lewis and Clark expedition spent on their travels really do differ greatly. In both cases the first chore for the men of the expedition was to construct shelter. In 1804 they built Fort Mandan near present day Washburn, North Dakota. In 1805 they erected Fort Clatsop along the Oregon Coast. Both named for nearby Indian tribes.

As you would expect the climate of the Oregon coast differed greatly from the plains of the Dakotas. Neither presented weather that we would consider conducive to an extended camping trip. The winter the Corp spent on the plains of the Dakotas was bitterly cold, compared to the warmer but wetter winter weather of the Pacific coast. One journal entry indicates that over the course of three weeks the skies were so overcast that sightings on the sun necessary for determining latitude and longitude were impossible.

Another entry laments the high humidity and the difficult task of drying hides and meats. Even the Corp of Discovery's tools and supplies were damaged by the constant rain and moisture. In fact their buckskin clothing and buffalo robe bedding rotted around them.

At Fort Mandan the members of the Lewis and Clark expedition spent a good deal of time with their Native American neighbors, trading blacksmith work for foods such as corn and buffalo meat. At Fort Clatsop there was less contact with the neighboring tribes and most of the trading that occurred was for salmon or occasionally dogs for meat.

The expedition's time on the Pacific Coast gave them a couple opportunities that weren't available on the prairies. Men were assigned the task of boiling down sea water to gather the salt that would be left. Over the course of the winter they made twenty gallons of the precious commodity needed to cure meat.

And the Oregon coast gave the Corps of Discovery one other opportunity that they would never get on the plains of the Dakotas. On January 8, 1806 Captain Lewis, Sacagawea and others traveled to a beached whale. There they traded with Indians who were harvesting the blubber of this 105 foot long find.

Wrong Side Up

John Christenson had emigrated from Germany to the United States at the age of nineteen. After traveling about a bit he ended up in Wisconsin working as a $14 a month farm hand. Quite often the wages were only paid during the summer with the farm laborers lucky to be able work for room and board through the winter. Not exactly wages that would allow him to realize his dream of a farm of his own.

But John got his chance for a place of his own through the German Evangelical Church of Chicago. They were organizing German immigrants to form a colony of farmers in western Dakota Territory near the present town of New Salem. For a $20 membership fee John Christenson became a colonist in the Dakotas.

When he arrived with the other German settlers there was no town or even depot to greet them. Planks were set up from the box cars to a nearby dirt bank to unload horses and wagons. The settlers first built some communal buildings and a church before dispersing to their own claims. Without springs or freshwater streams the only water available had to come from wells. These were hand dug, often eight feet across and as deep as forty feet.

John Christenson had the only plow in the community and broke sod for $5 an acre. He was working at this profession when he encountered two families of Indians. The men of the group stooped and turned the newly plowed sod back over to its original position. A young Indian traveling with the group translated their actions for an incredulous farmer by saying 'wrong side up, wrong side up'.

A plaque exists along highway 10 commemorating this encounter; it gives it credit for making New Salem the dairy region it is today. It stands as a monument not only to the settlers who came and faced the challenges of the prairie but to the Native Americans who saw their way of life changed forever.

Cards, Guns, and Petticoats

She started her career as a jig dancer in Texas. By the time she followed the boom to Deadwood in the Dakota Territory she had advanced herself to the status of professional gambler specializing in Faro. She also dressed in a scant gypsy girl costume as she dealt cards.

Her success at the turn of the card was quite phenomenal. Her Faro operation blossomed into a full fledged gambling house known as the 'Mint', an emporium that she not only used to lure in gamblers but husbands.

Husband number one won her hand when he was the only one of her lovers that would let her shoot an apple off his head while she rode past on her horse at a full gallop. History doesn't record what happened to this man but does note that he was followed quickly by four others.

In one instance she had vowed to shoot one of the regulars at the Mint. This gentleman wouldn't get into a gunfight with a woman, so Kitty Le Roy donned men's clothing and shot it out with him. Kitty's aim was true, her shot mortally wounding the man. In a fit of passion she married the man before he died, we don't know if this was husband number two, three, or four.

Not all of her husbands met a violent end. One German immigrant, and successful miner, was wooed by the pretty gambler. After he had spent his entire stake, some $8,000 in gold dust, Kitty broke a bottle over his head and ran him out of the Mint.

Many believe that more men were killed over Kitty Le Roy than all the other women in the Black Hills combined. In some cases jealousy among her lovers caused the shootings, at other times Kitty herself pulled the trigger.

But it was husband number five that ended the life and career of the Black Hills prettiest gambler. It may have been the most tragic of her many love affairs. Some say that he beat her to the draw in a fair shoot out, and then turned the gun on himself.

Pomp and Circumstance

Two centuries ago a little boy was born on the prairies of what is now North Dakota. A child that will travel the breadth of a continent before his second birthday. On February 11, 1805 the Corps of Discovery received its smallest and youngest member. Sacagawea's labor was considered 'tedious and violent' by the Captains. According to one of the translators with the expedition the natives used crushed rattlesnake rattles to ease childbirth.

Captain Lewis made a tea by crushing two rings of a rattle and gave it to the young mother-to-be. Within 10 minutes Jean Baptiste or 'Pomp' as he was more commonly referred to by the men of the expedition made his arrival into the world. For the rest of the expedition the child traveled on the back of his teenage mother.

The child, who was described as a happy, dancing baby boy, was a favorite of the members of the Lewis and Clark Expedition. Captain Clark even named a rock formation in what is now Montana for the child, christening it Pompey's Pillar. On the return trip Captain Clark took time to carve his name into this monument, the only visible mark of the Corps of Discovery still remaining.

Before her death in 1812 Sacagawea and her husband turn over to Clark not only their son but a newborn daughter. General Clark adopted the children. Although it is assumed the girl died in infancy the boy was raised and educated in the finest schools. Pomp went to work for the Missouri Fur company in 1821 and while traveling in the Rocky Mountains met and befriended a German Duke who took him to Europe and continued his education there.

Able to speak English, German, Spanish and French as well as several Indian dialects Jean Baptiste is one of the best educated of the Mountain Men when he returned to the American West. His adventures include trapping and trading in the Rockies, guiding the Mormon Battalion to California, serving as an interpreter for various government explorations and finally as a gold miner during the California gold rush.

Jean Baptiste Charbonneau died in 1866 in Oregon; he was headed for another adventure, this time in the Montana Gold Fields.

Fool Soldiers to the Rescue

The Uprising of the Sioux along the Minnesota River in August of 1862 was one of the most violent and bloody periods of frontier history. Some of the captives of this terrible episode traveled hundreds of miles before their rescue. In fact two women and a group of children ended up along the Missouri River near present day Mobridge, South Dakota in the fall of that year.

Mrs. Duly, Mrs. Wright, their children and three other children were known as the Shetak captives and had been forced by their captors hundreds of miles west from their homes along Shetak Lake in southern Minnesota to the shores of the big Muddy River.

For these unfortunate women and children their rescue from the Sioux came from an unusual source. Many of the young Sioux men were members of warrior societies. One of these secret groups was known to the whites as the 'Fool Soldiers' and were led by Martin Charger. Early reports speculated that the Fool Soldiers were dedicated to helping the whites, possibly due to Charger's grandfather being Captain Lewis of Lewis and Clark fame, though no historic research confirms this relationship. Others believe that their strong belief in Lakota principles of honor prohibited them from making war against women and children.

In any case they came to the rescue of Mrs. Duly and Mrs. Wright and the children, trading for them along the Missouri near present day Mobridge, South Dakota. On a cold day in late November, 1862 the captives were presented to their rescuers, naked. The women and children were wrapped in blankets and loaded on horses and travois for a hurried trip south to Fort Pierre.

The Fool Soldiers would later serve as the nucleus of the Indian Police. Many would also enlist in the United States Army, the only non-whites allowed to serve along side white soldiers in this country's wars from the Spanish-American War to the early days of the Korean Conflict when the military became fully integrated.

The City of Swans

With few exceptions the early occupants of the forts along the Missouri River during the 1860's and 70's were 100% male. The posts were considered too rough, rugged and even dangerous for the wives of the officers. Even laundresses, women paid from money withheld from the soldiers pay for washing their uniforms, were not common at places like Forts Buford, Stevenson, Rice or Sully.

Most of these posts had few of the features that we now consider necessities. Little things like indoor bathing facilities or even a steady supply of water didn't exist at these frontier forts. The perception of the climate of the Dakotas also kept many of the fairer sex at bay. The Dakota weather was described as a combination of 'Death Valley and Alaska'. And while most of these forts had small libraries and games like billiards and croquet the most common recreation of the soldiers and officers seemed to be alcohol.

But by the late 1860's the forts in southern Dakota were becoming a little more civilized. A report from Dr. Bean, an army surgeon who visited Fort Sully, near present day Pierre, South Dakota, stated that the post was comfortable. The doctor continued that the presence of nine or ten women, most likely the wives of officers, made the post 'more pleasant and society more refined'.

But wives and laundresses were not the only women who came to the forts. Near Fort Randall a small village sprang up called 'White Swan City'. The city was named for the two women, the 'white swans' that made their living there although most would have referred to them by another aviary reference. Most would have called them soiled doves.

The White River Cure

The White River in western South Dakota got its name from the milky color of the water. This tint comes from the white clay sentiments that the river picks up as it courses its way through the badlands.

The river has had many names through the years, White Earth River, Smoky Earth River and White Clay Creek to name a few. It seems to always have been known for some of its other qualities.

James Clyman, a hunter with the Ashley Brigade in 1824, wrote about his time in the area as the party traveled west to the Yellowstone River Valley to trap. He relates that their guide told them not to drink too much of the water from the White River because too much could cause constipation. Clyman also tells us that many in the party had a drink and that it worked just as the guide had warned.

I doubt that any of that party of hunters 180 years ago thought about the 'binding quality' of the water as anything but an inconvenience. They should have looked at those waters as medicinal.

Clays very similar to those that flow naturally in the White River are used in anti-diarrhea medicines such as Kaopectate today. The White River, where a drink of water wouldn't keep you going.

A Really Shortline

Less than a mile and a quarter long, the Wahpeton – Breckenridge Street Railway Company is really just a hop and a skip when compared to the other railroads of the time. In fact it is considered the shortest interstate rail line in the country. But from 1910 to 1925 it served as the easiest way to travel between these two Red River communities.

The yellow streetcars started their runs at 6 in the morning Monday through Saturday and at 7 on Sundays and operated until 11:30 in the evening. Fares started at just a nickel per trip, but were later raised to seven cents.

Powered by overhead electric lines the cars could hit a top speed of nearly twenty miles per hour. However, stops at any street corner with perspective passengers slowed the average speed considerably. A round trip from western Wahpeton to Eastern Breckenridge and back, a distance of less than two and half miles, took a half hour.

While the streetcars served people of all walks of life, in 1912 it averaged nearly 800 passengers per day, there was always speculation about who financed and benefited most from the railway.

During much of the period when the streetcars traveled through Wahpeton, North Dakota and Breckenridge, Minnesota prohibition existed on the West side of the River. Many people speculated that the streetcar company was financed by the taverns on the east side of the river.

Speculation at least partially fueled by the name of the bar along the line closest to the Red River. The First and Last Chance Saloon was aptly named. If you were headed east it was your first chance for a stiff drink, if you were going west it was your last 'shot' for a 'shot'. The streetcars ceased to operate in 1925, derailed by the wider use of cars and the cost of maintaining rails in the newly paved streets.

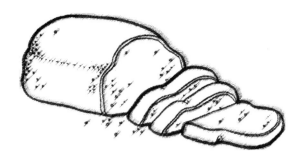

But Captain What Will We Put on the Toast?

While the Corps of Discovery was not discovering anything new, the rivers, hills, and cliffs of the American West were well known to the Native Americans who made their homes there, they were the first Americans to see these sights. That gave them the honor of mapping and assigning names to all the places they found.

In some cases they used names already established by the French traders who had traveled the area for years. The Vermillion and Cheyenne Rivers of South Dakota come to mind. Other places were named for members of the expedition. In Iowa you can visit Floyd Creek and Floyd Hill named for the only member of the expedition to perish on the trail.

Some rivers were named for politicians; the Jefferson and Madison are still prominent trout streams in Montana. And some were even named for girls that were left behind, the Marias River was named by Captain Lewis for his cousin Maria Wood and the Judith is named by Captain Clark for a girl back east that he hoped to marry on his return.

But some of the names established were a little more whimsical. This characteristic seemed to be generally used on the islands of the Missouri River that they encountered. I think that we can assume that the Captains knew that the constant erosion caused by the swift river waters would erase these islands from the face of the earth if not from the maps the Corp created.

It's really too bad that these river islands are gone. If they hadn't washed away decades ago we could travel to central South Dakota and visit 'No Preserves Island', where on September 5th of 1804 the Lewis and Clark expedition ran out of jelly.

Love, Murder and Horses

It really all started as a love triangle on the Rosebud Reservation. One of the chiefs, Spotted Tail, fell in love with the wife of another of the chiefs, Crow Dog. This was not something that Crow Dog would tolerate. In August of 1881 Crow Dog shot and killed Spotted Tail.

A tribal court acquitted the accused at least partially due to the alienation of affection that Crow Dog had suffered in the incident. While this might have been the end of the case the authorities at the Indian Department brought charges in Federal Court. Deputy U.S. Marshal George Bartlett brought Crow Dog to Deadwood for trial.

The case dragged so long that the accused became a regular fixture at the jail and even became trusted enough to be released to do chores around town. At one point he even left word to tell the marshal that he was going to see family on the Pine Ridge reservation and that he'd be back in a few days. When Bartlett went after him Crow Dog found a fast horse and got back to Deadwood ahead of the pursuing lawman, greeting him with a smile through the bars of a jail cell after the ride.

Federal Court jurors found Crow Dog guilty of the murder of Spotted Tail and sentenced him to death by hanging. This verdict was appealed to the United States Supreme Court.

The justices in Washington D.C. overturned the lower court's ruling. They found that the Federal District Court in Deadwood lacked jurisdiction over a crime committed on a reservation. They also ruled that Crow Dog had given enough ponies to the victim's family as retribution effectively ending the case.

Park It Over There

Efforts for a National Park or Monument in the North Dakota Badlands to former resident and President Theodore Roosevelt go back to the 1920's. The early lobbying was sidelined first by the depression and drought of the 1930's and World War II. It is not until after peace is won that serious consideration is given to idea of a National Park in western North Dakota. North Dakota Congressman Lemke introduced the legislation creating the park in 1945, it passed in 1946 but was vetoed by President Truman.

Lemke reintroduced similar legislation on January 9, 1947. The boundaries of the park were enlarged to include Roosevelt's Elkhorn Ranch and the name of the park, a contentious issue, was deferred until later. Some federal officials felt that the area did not meet the criteria of a National Park but rather should be designated a Monument. A compromise was reached in the form of the title 'Theodore Roosevelt Memorial Park'.

With that detail worked out Congress passed and President Harry Truman signed the legislation creating Theodore Roosevelt Memorial National Park in April of 1947.

The park boundary and a few other details continued to be debated and amended through the next few years. Originally the park plan included a monument to Teddy in the town of Medora and was considerably smaller. The dedication ceremony was held at Painted Canyon on June 4, 1949. Estimates run as high as 40,000 people attending.

Park Headquarters were at the Peaceful Valley Ranch. The new park's inventory included some World War II surplus fire fighting equipment, trucks and a road grader.

The park's avowed purpose was to recreate the open range landscape of the days of Theodore Roosevelt, but they planned to do this without any domestic livestock. In early December of 1953 officials ordered all cattle removed from within park boundaries by the end of the year.

The next spring officials turned their attention to the wild horses roaming Theodore Roosevelt Memorial Park. These animals were not the true mustangs of western lore but instead animals strayed or released by depression era farmers and ranchers of the region.

From April 30th through May 2nd of 1954 local cowboys and park rangers combined to roundup all the horses in the park. This event had enough of a western flavor to attract the attention of the national press. Reporters from the New York Times and Minneapolis Tribune told the world about the roundup and the North Dakota Badlands.

Man the Lifeboats

Oscar Hedman had emigrated from Sweden to the United States in 1905. For the next seven years he worked as a farmer and hotel clerk settling in Bowman, North Dakota. He was also employed by a St. Paul real estate company to recruit Scandinavian settlers to join him here in the Dakotas. This job had taken him back to Sweden in October of 1911.

While there Hedman convinced seventeen people to follow him back to the United States. These people must have boarded the ship for the cross Atlantic trip with anticipation. After all, they were headed for a new life in a new country. Unfortunately it was a trip that most would not complete.

Oscar Hedman and his followers had booked their passage on the White Star Liner, the Titanic. As we all know on April 14, 1912 the ship struck an ice berg and sank that night with over 1600 people losing their lives. Hedman claimed to be one of the last people to dive off the doomed liner minutes before it sank, he was taken into a lifeboat after a crewman on board had fallen overboard and was lost.

Of the seventeen perspective settlers headed for Bowman it appears only three survived, none of whom came to the Dakotas. When Oscar arrived in New York he was advanced $10 by the Women's Relief Corp who also helped him arrange passage to company headquarters in Minnesota.

Oscar Hedman finally arrived home on May 9th, less than one month after the tragedy. He told the Bowman County Pioneer that he had enough of the ocean and never expected to trust himself to it again.

In his later life he worked as a self-trained chiropractor, sometimes at odds with health officials in South Dakota. He died in Onida, South Dakota in 1961 at the age of 77, truly a survivor.

Death and Taxes

Government and taxation go hand in hand and the early days of the Dakota Territory were no exception. The first Territorial Legislature in 1862 set about implementing the taxes that would finance the operations of the territory.

They determined that all privately owned land in the territory was to be taxed along with personal property such as ferry boat franchises, toll bridges, cattle, horses, mules, asses, sheep, swine, money, either bank deposits or cash, and household furniture valued at not more than $100.

The process, as instituted in 1862, was that each county would elect an assessor who would visit and appraise the property. This would be the basis for the calculation of the taxes.

The system of taxes seemed quite complete except for one thing. There was no method of enforcement. In fact, two years later territorial Governor Edmunds called the tax law 'dead letters on the statute books' because no taxes had yet been collected. The 1864 legislature did not put any teeth in tax collections. In 1865 Edmunds asked the territorial assembly again to make taxes mandatory. The territory's auditor and treasurer had not been paid in four years and were owed nearly $400 in back wages.

To make matters worse a shipment of books and journals from the Library of Congress had been sent to the new territory freight collect. Without $160 in the territorial bank account to pay the charges, the literature couldn't be received.

The indifference to finances by the territorial assembly might have come from Washington. The federal statute that formed the territory appropriated $40,000 for the operation of the Territorial Legislature for two years. Many felt this money would be sufficient to operate the entire government. However, the money was only used for the expenses of the assembly. The members of those early congresses in Yankton got paid but many of the other bills of the government were left delinquent.

The 1866 legislature set the tax rate at five mills on real and personal property supplemented by a one dollar per person poll tax on voters. The rates were sufficient to get the territory out of the red ink and into the black. They also ended a nearly five year period where death may have been a certainty but taxes weren't in the Dakota Territory.

We're Looking for Mr. D. Boone

In the late 1700's Daniel Boone and his son led a colony of their fellow Kentuckians onto a Spanish Land Grant in the Louisiana Territory. The Boone farmstead and its surrounding village was forty or fifty miles up the Missouri from St. Louis.

On May 24, 1804, just eight days into the expedition, the Corps of Discovery stopped by for a little visit. It would have been interesting to hear a conversation between Daniel Boone and the Captains Lewis and Clark. Boone would have been 62 at the time of the meeting, his entire life spent on the frontier exploring the woods of Kentucky and other places.

But it is unlikely that this trio of the greatest explorers of the American West ever met. Clark's journal states that a number of people greeted them at the river bank when they came ashore. He continues that they purchased some corn and butter but makes no mention of meeting the great frontiersman. There are no surviving journal entries from Captain Lewis for the day.

It is possible that Boone would have looked on the American expedition with a little resentment. He could be considered one of the great losers in the Louisiana Purchase. Now part of the United States his land grants were subject to court action for unpaid debts in Kentucky. Most of his property was seized.

But where was Daniel Boone two hundred years ago when Lewis and Clark came to call. My guess is he was out hunting and exploring, activities he continued for nearly twenty more years until his death in 1820.

It's too bad; any words of advice from Daniel Boone to the Corps of Discovery would have been priceless as they explored the Missouri and the American West. The expedition continued on its way. They stopped the next day at La Charrette, a small village along the Missouri that would be the last white outpost they would encounter until they returned in 1806.

Marching on Their Stomachs

The 1863 march north along the Missouri River for General Sully and his troops had been plagued by problems. Drought and the low river levels it caused had delayed steamboats of supplies causing Sully to be fully a month late as he rode towards a rendezvous with General Sibley near present day Bismarck, North Dakota.

When he finally started the march it was during the heat of the summer and plagued by hail storms and prairie fires. The rations for a traveling army of the day would have included beans, salt pork and hard tack. This rather repetitive diet would make anyone yearn for a thick fresh broiled steak.

On August 24, 1863, about a day's march or 20 miles south of present day Bismarck, North Dakota, they encountered a large herd of buffalo. General Sully ordered a party of cavalry troopers out to hunt fresh meat for the camp.

It is possible these troops decided to have a little sport by hunting buffalo Indian style. This would involve riding at a gallop along side the running beast and firing nearly point blank into the chest of the running animal. This was certainly more thrilling than shooting from long distance but also much more dangerous.

Unfortunately, things did not go smoothly on this little hunting trip. General Sully's reports do not indicate what difficulties his troops encountered but he does state, in his official military report, that the hunting party was recalled because they were disabling more horses than buffalo.

But the General's attention quickly turned from bison to Indians. The next day his scouts captured several Indians and learned that Sibley had returned to Minnesota a month earlier. Sully made a swing to the east on his return and fought the battle of Whitestone Hill on September 3rd and 5th.

Head Em Up and Move Em Out

During the last years of the era of open range ranching roundups became larger and larger. There are several candidates for the honor of the largest organized gather of livestock to ever take place.

Some of the candidates for the roundup honors include a Texas Panhandle gather that brought in 25,000 cattle. This pales in comparison to a Wyoming roundup that put together a final herd of nearly 200,000 beefs although this gather had a number of different foremen as ramrod.

Some stockmen consider the Killdeer Mountain Roundups in North Dakota in the late 1800's as large or larger than any of these but according to Ed Lemmon in his autobiography 'Boss Cowman' he managed the largest roundup of cattle ever.

In the spring of 1897 on the Peno Flats near the headwaters of the Bad River in western South Dakota, Lemmon bossed a crew made up of fifteen chuck wagons with a total of 300 working cowboys as they scoured the open range to gather more than 45,000 head of cattle.

After the herd was brought together every head had to be looked at by the 60 'reps' along the roundup. These were the representatives of the ranches in the roundup area there to tally the livestock found with their brands.

The open range days ended in the early years of the 20th century. The big roundups with thousands of cattle and horses worked by hundreds of men are now a century in the past. Barbed wire fences have broken the open range into pastures and motorcycles and all terrain vehicles often take the place of horses in driving cattle. It may be more efficient but it sure is a lot less romantic.

One Ringee Dingee

The hundred or so ranchers scattered across the thousand or so square miles of western North Dakota and eastern Montana prairie had never dealt with busy signals, wrong numbers or telemarketers. Not at least until December 15, 1971 when they became the last large area of residents in the continental United States to receive phone service.

With national news media in attendance, the first phone call ever made from Squaw Gap, North Dakota was long distance. They called Earl Butz in Washington D.C. the Secretary of Agriculture who oversaw the Rural Electrification Administration that had been instrumental in financing the new phone service.

The total cost of construction came to over $430,000 or $4,300 per family served. This amounted to seven times the national average cost. Costs that would have been prohibitive if not for low interest government loans.

For the next few days the national news media feasted on the little town with the new phones. A New York City radio station called to see how many buildings were in Squaw Gap, they were told six if you counted the new dial house for the phone service and both outhouses.

But the Wall Street Journal had the cruelest interpretation of the story. Their headline read 'It is Now Possible to Call Squaw Gap, But Who'd Want To'. The article drew a written response from Governor Guy and a fictitious Squaw Gap Chamber of Commerce that speculated that the Mayor of New York must be in the underwear business because he was having so much trouble with Union Suits.

The Squaw Gap Chamber went on to say that they couldn't understand the race riots in New York. They had only one race in Squaw Gap, usually on the Fourth of July.

For a few days, until the novelty wore off, the whole country was talking about the new phones ringing in the homes of western North Dakota. Homes that now had to deal with telemarketers.

The Journey Begins

The previous winter had been spent in the final preparations for the journey of the Corps of Discovery. The original plan of the expedition included a crew of just 15 men. As spring approached at St. Louis the roster had swollen to 56 men and a dog requiring a great deal of additional provisions.

Through this winter of preparation Captain Clark had lived with the men of the expedition in the crude cabins of Camp Dubois. Captain Lewis had spent the winter in the relative luxury of the home of Auguste Chouteau, a member of one of the founding families of St. Louis. Auguste's brother Pierre will operate fur trading posts along the Missouri River in later years.

Originally scheduled for mid April the departure of the Corps of Discovery had been delayed as supplies were added. Additional flour and whiskey were added and billed to the War Department. Changes were also made to the Keel Boat to make it more defendable. A canon was added to the bow and a swivel blunderbuss was mounted on the stern just in case they needed to repel boarders.

But on May 14, 1804 all the planning and preparation came to fruition. At 4pm the Keel Boat and Pirogues started their journey up the Missouri River under the command of Captain Clark. That first day they made just four miles and camped on an island. Clark's journal states that the men were in high spirits after finally getting under way.

Two days later the expedition paused at St. Charles where the cargo of the keel boat was adjusted so the vessel would ride better on the snag plagued Missouri. And there Captain Lewis caught up with his partner and crew as well. He had remained behind wrapping up some last minute details like forwarding his mail. Any letters for Meriwether Lewis sent to St. Louis were to be forwarded to President Jefferson to hold until he returned from his journey, a trip that will cross the continent and take nearly three years to complete.

Self Defense on the Back Roads

Roy Michaelson listed his occupation as a professional boxer from Minneapolis, Minnesota. His record in sanctioned bouts was one win, one loss, and one draw. In all likelihood he fought in many unsanctioned fights across the midwest in his brief stint in the ring.

In late 1930 his career had brought him to Merricourt, North Dakota. There he became friends with the local moon shiners, the Brossart Brothers, spending the holidays and the first weeks of 1931 at their farm northwest of town. On January 12, 1931 three Brossart Brothers, John Ellingson, and the boxer Roy Michaelson robbed Jenner Merchandise in downtown Merricourt. While no one witnessed the crime a local Gas Station attendant noticed the Brossart car at the store late on a Saturday night. When the robbery was discovered on Sunday morning Dickey County Sheriff B. W. Crandall was called and after a brief chase arrested the Brossarts, Ellingson, and Michaelson and recovered $500 in stolen merchandise. The sheriff also discovered fifteen gallons of illegal booze at the farm.

On the trip to the jail at Ellendale the Brossarts and Ellingson were put in the deputy's car. The pro boxer, Roy Michaelson was the only prisoner transported in the Sheriff's car. While the two cars left together they became separated and were not traveling together as they approached Ellendale. According to Sheriff Crandall, two miles out of Ellendale the prisoner tried to overpower him, forcing the car into the ditch. In a brief struggle the sheriff was forced to shoot and kill Roy Michaelson. While local speculation questioned whether the shooting was actually self-defense a local coroner's inquest convened two days after the incident ruled it a justifiable homicide.

Let it Burn

Sir George Gore put together quite a hunting party in 1854. After all, they were intent on taking a two year excursion into the American West. But the equipment and manpower that Sir Gore assembled exceeds what any of us could imagine.

Of course, Gore and some of his hunting companions traveled in fine carriages. Along with these carriages were Conestoga Wagons loaded with hunting and fishing equipment and camp equipment that included fine tablecloths, imported wine, and a complete library.

Guiding the expedition was renowned Mountain Man Jim Bridger. The party also included a number of armors to tend to the seventy five hunting rifles and one person whose sole responsibility was tying flies for the fishermen in the group.

Gore's hunting party was not always welcomed by the Native population. The Crow and other tribes of the Upper Missouri complained that they were decimating the wildlife population. Gore himself boasted of killing over 100 bear, 2000 buffalo, and 1600 elk, just for sport, during his two years on the plains.

The expedition journeyed from the Powder and Yellowstone Valleys to Fort Union, near present day Williston, North Dakota, in 1856. From there they intended to travel by sternwheeler to St. Louis and then home to Europe.

Sir Gore offered the wagons and equipment for sale at Fort Union for what he felt was a reasonable price. The traders at the fort, possibly because there were no other possible buyers in the region, offered just a small fraction of that price as a counter offer.

This angered the Irish Lord, instead of selling the wagons and supplies for what he felt was a ridiculously low price he burned them. Sir George had all the wagons, including his fine carriage, and all the equipment they didn't wish to take with them back to Europe piled in front of the fort gates and torched. He even posted guards around the conflagration to keep anyone from salvaging anything.

Gore only saved his rifles and hunting trophies, he even burned his own journals of the trip. The total cost of the two year adventure in the American West was $250,000, this back in a time when a quarter of a million dollars was still real money. Sir George Gore returned to Ireland and died in Inverness, Scotland in 1878.

The Indians Aren't Coming

Tensions on the Dakota Frontier were high. In 1862 the Santee Sioux had attacked settlers along the Minnesota River. As a result the United States Army took to the fields of the Dakotas in 1863, 64, and 65.

During this time a series of outposts were established from near Devils Lake south along the James River to central South Dakota. These camps were manned by Sisseton Sioux who had enlisted to serve with the Army. This force of scouts was headquartered at Fort Sisseton; in 1865 Samuel Brown was made its commander.

In April of 1866 he received word that tracks of hostile Indians had been found along the James River near present day LaMoure, North Dakota. He wrote a message to be sent the next day warning Fort Abercrombie and then saddled up and headed west to warn the other outposts.

It took him all day to travel 55 miles west of Fort Sisseton to the scouts posted near present day Ordway, South Dakota. The Indians there informed him that the tracks were not made by hostiles but by a peace party headed for the Missouri River.

Fearing that his dispatch to Fort Abercrombie would foster unnecessary panic Samuel Brown saddled a fresh horse and started back to Fort Sisseton yet that evening. During the return ride freezing rain turned to snow and finally blizzard conditions. At sunrise he determined the wind and snow had pushed him twenty miles south of the fort.

By the time the exhausted Brown rode his exhausted horse into Fort Sisseton he had ridden nearly 150 miles in 24 hours. He spread the word that the Indians weren't coming and then collapsed. He would never recover from the combination of exhaustion and exposure. His legs remained partially paralyzed for the rest of his life.

Brown lived his later life in Minnesota; the community of Brown's Valley is named in his honor.

Which Rock Should It Be?

South Dakota State Historian Doane Robinson should be credited with the idea of a mammoth stone carving in the Black Hills. He pictured a series of rock statutes to western figures such as General Custer, Kit Carson, Sioux Warriors and others. He turned to the only sculptor working on such a grand scale, Gutzon Burglum.

Burglum had been working on the Confederate Memorial Monument in Georgia for nine years. The project had been plagued by a shortage of funds, bickering among its executive board and other problems. He jumped at a chance to tour the Black Hills and talk about new opportunities.

His departure from the confederate project was not without controversy. Burglum destroyed his working models and left Georgia with the state's highway patrol in hot pursuit. He even claimed that he was shot at by the officers before he reached the safety of North Carolina.

Once in South Dakota Burglum immediately vetoed the idea of western heroes as subject matter. He specified that his masterpiece would be of national importance.

In September of 1924, after an extensive tour of the Black Hills and its rock formations, the artist made his decision. His vision was to sculpt a standing George Washington and Abraham Lincoln side by side just below the summit of Harney Peak, the highest point between the Rockies and the Swiss Alps.

The dedication of the project occurred in 1927. By that time the artist's vision had changed. Instead of two standing presidents the sculpture had grown to four busts and instead of Harney Peak the project was sited at Mt. Rushmore. The last fourteen years of Gutzon Burglum's life was spent in creating the Mt. Rushmore monument, a monument of national importance.

Let's Get this Expedition on the Road

It had been a long and cold winter at Fort Mandan but spring weather brought an opening of the river and the need to renew the journey of the Corps of Discovery. But April 7, 1805 also brought changes to the makeup of the expedition.

The fifty foot long keelboat, now crewed by six soldiers and two French boatmen, started downriver to return to St. Louis. The boat carried the maps, journals and specimens collected by the Captains Lewis and Clark the previous summer. With the strong spring current of the Missouri at their back they anticipated an easy trip.

For the two officers, three sergeants, twenty three privates, two interpreters, one slave, one woman, one baby, and one dog remaining in what has been referred to as the permanent party it was time to head west. The two pirogues, one red and one white, were supplemented by six canoes to carry the men and equipment on the next leg of the expedition.

While there were fewer people gathered to witness their departure from Fort Mandan than from St. Louis the previous spring you could say that they were now departing into the wilderness. Many expeditions, both French and Spanish as well as independent traders, had traveled as far as the Mandan Villages in what is now North Dakota. Lewis and Clark had even read translations of the journals of McKay and Evans who had wintered with the Mandan in the late 1790's.

But now the Corps of Discovery traveled into uncharted territory. The only existing maps of the upper Missouri were based on the oral reports of the Native Americans of the region. Over the next year they will visit areas that no white men had traveled through and record places, plants and animals that were unknown to scientists and geographers.

Their expedition opens the American northwest, first to the fur traders and trappers of the Mountain Man era and then to the ranchers and homesteaders that followed, a pretty big accomplishment for such a small band of travelers.

A Bridge Over Muddy Waters

In 1840 Stephen Riggs was already an experienced missionary to the Indians of the Plains. He and his wife, Mary, had been part of the Presbyterian efforts to bring the gospel to the Sioux in western Minnesota for 3 years.

In the fall of 1840 Stephen Riggs was sent on a mission. He and fellow teacher Alexander Huggins traveled from their homes along the Minnesota River west to the Missouri River at Fort Pierre Choteau. They had been directed to determine if the Sioux in the western Dakotas were ready to be missioned to.

Even though Riggs and Huggins were well received, a feast was even held in their honor, the Sioux weren't ready to receive the Gospel or the ministers preaching it. The duo returned to Minnesota a month later.

In later years Riggs' sons, Alfred and Thomas are instrumental in starting the first missions and schools to the Sioux on the Missouri River Reservations.

On June 28, 1926 a bridge across the Missouri between Pierre and Ft. Pierre was dedicated to Stephen Riggs. The bridge was probably within sight of the hill where Riggs had preached his sermon more than 86 years earlier.

The Stephen Return Riggs Bridge served as a vital link across the Missouri until 1962. During its first summer as many as a thousand vehicles a day crossed the bridge, a few even propelled by old fashioned horse power.

Today traffic crosses the Missouri on the Captain John C. Waldron Bridge just south of the site of the Riggs Bridge. Waldron was a Medal of Honor winner from South Dakota who was killed in World War II.

If We Can't Invade Canada, Let's Go West

Michael Quinn was born in Ireland in 1846 and immigrated to the United States in 1864. However, he does not come to the Dakotas until 1876 when he begins operations as a freighter between Cheyenne, Wyoming and Deadwood. Later he moves his business to the east side of the Hills and operates wagons between Pierre and Deadwood. He also began a cattle ranch along the Cheyenne River that ultimately became his sole enterprise.

In 1892, when reservation land along the Bad River was opened to settlement, Quinn moved his herd. The rest of his life was dedicated to the operation and expansion of this spread as well as his business interests in the area. He was such a major force in the region that a new community, founded in 1907, was named Quinn in his honor.

But what had Michael Quinn been doing in the years between his immigration and his arrival in the Dakotas? He had worked as a freighter on the trails to Fort Laramie and Denver for many years but before that he had been involved in a little international intrigue.

During his early years in America he had become part of the Fenian Brotherhood, a band of Irish ex-patriots that vowed to fight the English anywhere in the world as a way of advancing Ireland's independence.

In 1866, just two years after Michael Quinn arrived on these shores, he took part in the Fenian invasion of Canada through the state of Maine. While the invasion has some initial successes it is repelled by Canadian Militia and forced back into the United States.

That's right, the man for whom Quinn, South Dakota is named, once invaded Canada.

Mister Chairman

While territorial status had been conveyed on the area in March of 1861 it was a full year before there was any locally elected government in the region. When the Territorial Assembly did convene it was called 'Wide-open, red-hot, and mighty interesting' by the papers of the day.

It was referred to as the 'pony congress' because of its small size. You didn't need a lot of elected representatives; the population of the territory was just over 2300 people although many of the Métis that lived near Pembina probably had been out on a buffalo hunt when the census takers had called.

Yankton had been chosen by Governor Jayne as a temporary capital, possibly at the urging of Mary Todd Lincoln who hoped to benefit her cousin, John Todd, who was active in Yankton area politics as well as the real estate market.

But that first assembly did not get under way with a full slate of delegates. Hugh Donaldson was five days late in arriving after making the 400 mile trip from Pembina by dog sled.

And that first territorial assembly could only be referred to as 'rowdy'. Over the course of the debates the Speaker of the House, George Pinney, was thrown through a saloon window by the Sergeant-at-Arms, Jim Somers. Somers would not be a stranger to violence; he died in a gunfight in Chamberlain a few years later.

Despite the rough and rowdy ways of this assembly they did accomplish a great deal. During their sixty day session they defined eighteen counties, organized a militia to defend against attacks by Indians or Confederates, outlawed prostitution and gambling, and prohibited hogs and stallions from being allowed to run at large.

Not a bad accomplishment for an assembly that, according to one report, allowed the firing of a pistol shot to get the chairman's attention during debates.

A Five Hundred Century Old Park

Ole S. Quammen was a Norwegian immigrant who had settled and prospered in northwestern South Dakota. His business interests included lumber yards and gas stations in the Lemmon area but it was his amateur interest in geology that helped him make his biggest mark in the region.

In 1930 Ole hired two crews of men to gather petrified wood and construct a most unique park in his adopted home town of Lemmon. The city was a logical choice, nowhere else in the United States is petrified wood as plentiful.

For two years the crews labored gathering what seemed like an unlimited supply of the rare stones. They were constructed into cones, pyramids and even a castle. The tallest structure stands more than 32 feet tall. The floor of the castle was made entirely of petrified grass. Many of the structures weigh hundreds of tons. In some cases a single petrified log weighed as much as 10,000 pounds.

We can assume that the men, thirty or forty during the height of construction, were thankful for the work during the early years of the depression.

This unique monument was dedicated on June 2, 1932. Nearly 10,000 people attended the ceremony which featured a parade of marching bands, floats, some of which featured local products like coal, beef cattle, and even baby chicks, and celebrities like the governor.

Over the years the Petrified Wood Park has been expanded to include a local museum, also constructed of petrified wood, and Ole Quammen's gas station has now been turned into a gift shop and interpretive center.

Ole Quammen died just two years after the completion of his park. His lasting mark on the community constructed of materials that were at least 50,000 years old.

Giving Peace a Chance

Even in 1915 the conflict in Europe was bloody. Estimates put the cost in human lives at nearly 20,000 per day. This led multi-millionaire Henry Ford to look for a way to bring peace to the continent. Ford had pledged that he would spend half his wealth if his efforts could shorten the war by just one day.

Ford chartered a ship and offered passage to hundreds of American leaders to make a trip to the Scandinavian Countries. From there, with added strength from the Norwegian, Finnish, and Swedish leaders, the intent was to hold an international peace conference and end the Great War.

Invitations were sent to business and political leaders in November of 1915. The federal government refused to have any part in the peace mission, this prompted most elected officials to decline the trip.

In fact, the trip's only political leader was North Dakota's Republican Governor Louis Hanna. While many business leaders, men such as Edison and Carnegie, made the trip, political pressure had effectively stopped most elected officials from accepting.

The Peace Mission was widely viewed as a farce. Some newspapers editorialized that it was actually an advertising ploy for the Ford Motor Company. Internal disputes among the delegates plague the mission even before it reaches Norway.

But when the ship does reach Europe the press there looks for the highest ranking American government official as a leader. They find North Dakota Governor Louis Hanna.

The Governor himself has become disillusioned with Ford and the efforts of the mission. Hanna had made an earlier trip to Norway to deliver a statue of President Lincoln in 1914. When he called on old friends in government the Ford organization characterizes these visits as official acceptance by the Norwegian Government. Louis Hanna leaves the Ford Peace Mission over what he considers misinformation.

The Peace Mission is a failure. What we now know as World War I continues to rage across Europe until November of 1918. America becomes involved in the combat in 1917.

An Artist in all Mediums

Oscar Howe was born at Fort Thompson on the Crow Creek Reservation to a life of abject poverty. The Yanktonai Sioux youth's childhood was difficult. His father did not like his early attempts at art and sometimes took his pencils and paper away.

His early days of school were challenging. Even though he spoke only the Lakota language he was enrolled in the Indian Boarding School in Pierre that required only English be spoken.

But, oddly enough, health problems gave Oscar Howe his greatest opportunity. When diagnosed with tuberculosis he was sent to New Mexico to recuperate. While there he was enrolled in the Art Department of the Santa Fe Indian School. By the time of his graduation in 1935 his paintings were being shown in galleries across the country.

After service in World War II he returned to South Dakota and attended Dakota Wesleyan University before pursuing a graduate degree at the University of Oklahoma.

For a time Oscar Howe was angered by his inability to exhibit his works in some of the major eastern galleries. After his entry into the Philbrook Competition of 1958 was refused he wrote a letter accusing the eastern art society of treating Indian Artists like 'children' that needed to be guided. In 1959 not only was his entry accepted but won the Grand Purchase Prize.

In 1960 Howe was named the 'artist laureate' for the State of South Dakota. His works are displayed in fine galleries across the country and in public buildings in South Dakota including the Mitchell Library and Mobridge City Auditorium.

So what medium did this fine artist work? I don't know if he used oils, or pastels, or even acrylics for most of his paintings. But I do know that in at least one case he worked in 'corn'. Shortly after returning from service in World War II he designed and supervised that year's grain mural on the World Famous Corn Palace in Mitchell.

Poor health caused Howe to end his painting career in the mid 1970's. The University of South Dakota, where he taught in the art department for many years, has a large collection of his works. Many of his paintings are also exhibited at the 'Oscar Howe Memorial Arts Center' in Mitchell, South Dakota. He died in 1983.

The Cow Jumped Over the Moon

Burton 'Cap' Mossman, of Scottish descent born in Illinois, built an empire of grass and cattle in northwestern South Dakota through his own ambition and abilities.

While he started his ranching career in the American southwest, he managed the Hash-Knife Ranch for a time and earned his nickname of 'Cap' for his service as the first Captain of the Arizona Rangers, it was in South Dakota he made his mark.

His drive to expand the range of the ranch he managed was well-known among his cowboys and prompted at least the legend of this exchange between a couple of 'Diamond A' hands around the campfire.

One of the cowhands, getting a little philosophical as he watched the moon rise over the prairie wondered aloud if there was any grass, water or trees on the lunar surface.

His companion answered quickly and emphatically that he knew for a fact that there was no grass on the moon.

When pressed on how he could be so sure there was no life on the moon he stated, "If there was any grass up there Cap Mossman would have leased it for pasture years ago".

Mossman's Diamond A was quite certainly the largest ranch in South Dakota and among the largest in the nation. It totaled over a million acres and ran more than 50,000 head of cattle all in the northwest part of South Dakota covering parts of Stanley and Dewey counties. We have no confirmed history that he ever ran any cattle on the moon.

Mossman managed the Diamond A until 1944 when it was sold. He died in New Mexico in 1956 oddly enough at Roswell, a place known for its extraterrestrial activities.

Now We're in a Pickle

Fanny Kelly was taken captive by the Lakota when the wagon train she and her family were traveling with on the Bozeman Trail in eastern Wyoming was attacked. During her time with the Sioux she witnessed the Battle of Killdeer Mountain and a raid on an emigrant caravan traveling from Minnesota to the Montana Gold Fields.

While the Lakota had been defeated by General Sully at Killdeer Mountain despite the large gathering of the tribes there, they fared better against a wagon train in what is now the very southwest corner of North Dakota.

Sitting Bull's Hunkpapa surprised the gold seekers and managed to capture two wagon loads of supplies including several jars of pickles, the first that the Indians had encountered. Fanny Kelly describes the reaction by the Lakota to their first taste of the acidic cucumbers.

The Lakota made faces and decided that maybe the flavor would improve with cooking. They placed the pickles, still in the glass jars, directly in the camp fires. When the jars broke the Indians ridiculed the quality of these 'white man's kettles'.

Fanny Kelly's captivity lasted five months, she was returned in the winter of 1864 at Fort Sully in South Dakota. She wrote about her ordeal in a book entitled 'Narrative of My Captivity Among the Sioux Indians'. Kelly describes a life of fear and hardship at the hands of her captors. Terror that was only occasionally interrupted by the lighter side of the clash between the red and white cultures.

The Plague of 1918

A one stanza poem was often quoted in the newspapers of 1918.

>   I had a little bird
>   Its name was Enza
>   I opened up a window
>   And in flew Enza

During the last year of the First World War a dreaded disease made its annual appearance but this time with a viciousness that was unprecedented. What was referred to as the Spanish Influenza actually started in China. Through the summer of 1918 the disease progressed through Europe, infecting the American Doughboys stationed overseas.

By late summer many of the American posts both in Europe and America were infected. From there it spread to the civilian population and across the land. By late September the disease was common in the Dakotas.

On the 9th of October the North Dakota Health Department ordered all public places closed upon the recommendation of the Red Cross and War Department. The intent was to limit the spread of the disease by limiting the gathering of people. Despite these efforts the pandemic ran wild.

New Rockford, North Dakota reported over 100 cases of the disease. In Fargo as many as 300 cases would be documented in a single day. As the epidemic ran its course medical professionals became another casualty, by mid October, 27 nurses were sick in Jamestown.

In South Dakota the disease was first noted in mid September. Lennox, South Dakota, with a population of 900 in 1918 saw 52 people fall ill on October 3rd. Two people perished on the first day of the epidemic including the town's only physician.

A few days latter Pierre closed all schools while the disease ran its course there. All across both Dakotas not only were schools closed but all public gatherings were prohibited and people were urged to wear a gauze mask if they had to go to a store for any of the necessities of life.

Even funerals, and there were many as the disease progressed, were affected. The ban on public gatherings limited attendance to just the immediate family although outdoor graveside services were allowed.

Despite these efforts the disease continued to spread and ultimately affected over a quarter of the population. Nationally October was the deadliest month with five out of every one hundred Americans losing their lives. Hospitals were not equipped to handle these kinds of numbers of severely ill people. In Aberdeen, Graham Hall on the Northern State Campus was utilized as a makeshift hospital.

The disease ran its course in a matter of months; by late October doctors in both Dakotas were noting a decrease in the number of cases. It was a needed respite from the death and suffering of the year. Globally an estimated 25 million people died of influenza. In America over 600,000 perished, more deaths than the combat of World War I, World War II, Korea and Viet Nam combined.

No Water in the Well, But Gold?

The February 2, 1904 Steele Ozone called it possibly one of the biggest Gold Strike ever, and it was right there in Kidder County near Steele, North Dakota. But it didn't start a stampede of prospectors to the area.

It would have been a little difficult for prospectors to pan for the gold that they claimed to have found. It was mixed with a layer of sand nearly 100 feet below the surface. Well drillers in the area were suspicious of the black sand that they encountered while drilling water wells in the area. Some were so suspicious they sent samples to assayers for analysis.

While many samples showed a trace of gold in the heavy black gray sand one test revealed an amazing 620 ounces of gold per ton of ore. That equated to over $12,000 worth of gold in 1904 prices. The value of a ton of that sand now would approach a quarter of a million dollars.

The papers went on to say that the sand and gold were likely the bed of the ocean at some ancient time, long since covered by eons of sediment. An assumption that modern paleontology has proven correct.

The local newspapers promoted it extensively; the Steele Republican called it possibly one of the richest gold fields ever discovered. It is also a gold find that has gone unexploited.

My guess is that the pockets of gold rich sand proved too hit or miss for mining operations to be feasible. But for a few weeks the early settlers of Kidder County thought they were richer than the Klondike.

Oh, Say Can You See

Most people know that Francis Scott Key wrote the Star Spangled Banner, our National Anthem, as he watched the bombardment of Fort McHenry during the War of 1812. During the years that followed the poem was set to music and became a popular patriotic song even though it had no official status as our country's anthem.

More than one hundred years later, in 1916, President Woodrow Wilson ordered that the song be played at all official military functions. And in 1931 the United States Congress establishes the Star Spangled Banner as the official National Anthem of the United States.

But one military post was nearly forty years ahead of the pack in using the song for its formal ceremonies, or at least that is the claim of the Commander of Fort Meade in the Northern Black Hills. Colonel Caleb H. Carlson claims to have ordered the playing of the Star Spangled Banner as part of the post's official functions as early as 1892. Oddly enough the fort that may have the honor of being the first to use Francis Scott Keys' song in an unofficial capacity did not have an opportunity to be among the first to use it when the Army was ordered to use it. Fort Meade was temporarily abandoned from 1914 to 1917 and later served as a National Guard training base and a headquarters for the South Dakota branch of the Civilian Conservation Corps.

We now take it for granted that at the beginning of any sporting event or military event we'll hear the familiar refrain of the Star Spangled Banner but it must have been a novelty to stand on the parade grounds of old Fort Meade and hear 'Oh, say can you see'.

Medora Returns to Medora

On September 14, 1903 Medora de Mores returned to Medora, North Dakota. Actually, the de Mores earlier presence in the town that the Marquis had named after his wife was quite short. They originally arrived in 1882 with a dream of slaughtering cattle in the west and transporting the beef to the eastern markets in refrigerated rail cars. Over the next four years the Marquis will invest nearly 2 million dollars in the venture. Some of the funds represented his own wealth; Medora's father, a wealthy New York banker, invested as well.

Unfortunately the Marquis was a man ahead of his time. Transportation and refrigeration methods were too unreliable to transport the fresh meat reliably. In later years the idea of slaughtering animals near where they are raised will be the standard in the meat industry.

The Marquis and his family leave the Dakotas and the United States in 1886. Medora is widowed in 1895 when the Marquis is murdered in Africa while exploring routes for a railroad.

She does not return to this country and the town that bears her name until 1903 when she brings her children back to see where they had spent part of their youth. Her daughter, Athenaise and oldest son, Louis had both spent parts of their early childhood at the chateau on the hill overlooking Medora.

Medora had enjoyed the active lifestyle of the west during her years in the Dakota Territory. She was renowned as an avid horsewoman and hunter as well as being noted for her beauty. The Dickinson Press noted on her return that 'she had left a beautiful young woman' and 17 years later was 'still fine looking'.

Their stay is a brief but pleasant visit with old friends and acquaintances. The 18-year-old Louis only spends a few days before returning east to attend Yale University. Medora and her other children will spend several weeks at the chateau, ending their visit with a gala party at the Medora hall in October.

It's Dark Down in this Basement

In the fall of 1918 a gas leak at the Northern Pacific Depot in Jamestown, North Dakota made T. J. Ahearn suspicious. The manager of the local gas company found a valve open and a plug removed from the line. He was even more suspicious when a few hours after he made his repairs he was called back to the depot and found the same valve open and the same plug again removed.

With repairs made a second time Ahearn waited to return to the basement and investigate further. Two hours later there was still a smell of gas in the air when he lit a match to see the gas line better.

Fortunately Mr. Ahearn and the depot both survived the explosion and fire that ensued. Despite his injuries the gas company manager was able to report to the authorities and newspaper reporters his suspicion of German saboteurs at work in Jamestown in the late days of World War One. The Jamestown Alert reported that railroad detectives had been summoned and details on the plot would follow within 48 hours.

It was probably a natural assumption that the Northern Pacific Depot might be a target of sabotage. The building was new and the pride of the community, just two weeks earlier it had hosted former President Theodore Roosevelt during a brief whistle stop as he traveled the Northern Pacific line. But it was an assumption that was pure fantasy.

Two days later the Alert carried a letter from F. Ingalls, the District Manager for the NP Railroad. He stated that despite the sensationalism it was a case of ineptitude, not sabotage. An employee of the railroad had been sent to the basement to close a water line and drain it for the winter. He accomplished the task once then later in the day found that his work had been undone and was forced to repeat the job. History doesn't record the name of this railroad employee that couldn't tell a gas line from a water line, twice. But I think we can assume he wasn't the sharpest spike on the track. The letter from the NP manager wraps up with this statement, 'the explosion may not have been German propaganda but it did prove that the best way to find a leak in a gas line is to light a match.'

Riding the Line

The line camp in cattle country was a necessity in the days before fences. A line of camps, each roughly fifteen or twenty miles apart, was established along a boundary that area cattlemen wanted to keep their cattle from wandering across. Each of the camps would be manned by two cowboys through the winter, each morning they would ride off in opposite directions, herding any cattle back onto their own range. When they met the rider from the next camp up the line they would each turn back to their own place.

According to Theodore Roosevelt the ranchers of the Medora area cared little if their livestock drifted west or north but were concerned if the cattle drifted towards the east or southeast. They didn't want the herds to wander out of the rough country of the badlands into the farmlands to the east where they could do damage or be in danger.

The ranchers of the grazing association provided these camps that certainly would have varied widely in the level of comfort they provided for the two cowhands assigned to spend the winter there. Roosevelt said that some were mere tents pitched in a sheltered coulee, while the better line camps were either dugouts or log cabins. In either case a corral and horse shelter stood nearby.

Even Teddy, who enjoyed the outdoor life more than most, found the winter weather in the badlands challenging. Roosevelt stated that the cowboys needed to be out in wind and bitter cold turning back the herds. But even he admitted that during the worst of the weather it was impossible for anyone to be out tending the livestock.

These line camps became obsolete when the range was fenced with barbed wire. But during the days of the open range they provided winter work for the cowboys of the region. While most ranches hired quite a number of riders for the spring, summer, and fall work they would lay off the extra cowboys during the winter. Line camp duty was cold, isolated and dangerous, but the only work available through the winter for the cowboys of the Dakotas.

Take Two Mad Dog Plants and Call Me in the Morning

When Lewis and Clark made their historic journey up the Missouri nearly two centuries ago one of their tasks was to identify the new plants they found. One of the plants they encountered on the northern plains has since been given the name 'the narrow leaved or plains coneflower'.

The Corps of Discovery learned from the Indians the medicinal properties of the Coneflower and included a specimen in their shipment to President Jefferson in 1805 along with Mandan Tobacco and Arikara Beans.

Jefferson considered Mandan Tobacco vastly inferior to Virginia Tobacco and only suitable for cigars while the Arikara Beans were found to be very early maturing and quite tasty. But what about the coneflower?

I don't believe the President got a chance to test it. You see the Indians referred to the coneflower as the 'mad dog plant'. They used it as a treatment for people bitten by rabid dogs and rattle snakes.

Today the coneflower is better known as Echinacea and widely taken to improve immunity and ward off colds and flu, quite a difference from the early uses by Native Americans in treating the life threatening conditions of rabies and snake bite.

The State of Lincoln

North Dakota, South Dakota, and Lincoln, the state that almost was. Where would the state of Lincoln have been and how close did it come to actually being?

In the 1870's there were a number of plans to divide the Dakota Territory into smaller, more manageable segments. The existing territory was so large that many regions had little in common socially or economically.

In 1874 a proposal was made to divide the territory on a North and South basis with the new northern territory to be called the Pembina Territory. While this proposal received little consideration in Washington it did generate a lot of discussion here in the Dakotas.

In fact in 1877 another similar proposal surfaced. This time the plan was to divide the Dakota Territory on an East and West basis. The East would retain the name Dakota and the West would be christened the Lincoln Territory. This also did not receive much official consideration.

But the most aggressive plan came in 1878. Territorial Governor Howard called for the creation of three states from the existing territory. North Dakota and South Dakota would be defined much like they are currently with the exception that the Black Hills would form the third state of Lincoln. Governor Howard argued that all three regions were different economically and served by different railroad hubs.

None of these plans received much consideration outside the Dakotas. National politics would keep the serious discussion of Statehood off the floor of Congress until the late 1880's. By that time serious discussion was limited to the formation of a single state of Dakota or the North and South Dakota that we now know.

The One-Sided Shootout at LeBeau

LeBeau, South Dakota, came into existence to serve the ranches and the cowboys that they employed on the reservation leases west of present day Mobridge, South Dakota. In the early 1900's LeBeau boomed with a population of nearly 500 people.

As you would expect saloons were a common component of these western ranch communities. It is in the DuFran's Saloon in December of 1909 that violence erupted, an incident that will ultimately destroy the town.

David or Dode McKenzie was the manager of the Matador ranch as well as the son of Murdo McKenzie the ranch owner. As Dode entered the DuFran's Saloon the bar tender, Bud Stephens fired three shots, the first striking McKenzie in the chest, the next two struck him in the back as he spun back through the door. He died in the streets of LeBeau. Evidently a dispute going clear back to Texas had been resurrected by a rumor that McKenzie was gunning for Stephens. Stephens believed that he was shooting in self-defense.

The local cowboys were infuriated by the crime. When Stephens was acquitted of murder by a jury of town's people they boycotted the town of LeBeau. Bud Stephens was convinced by fellow townsmen to relocate for his own health but the worst blow came in 1910.

A fire devastated the business district, given the recent tension between the cowboys and the town arson was suspected. Also the fact that the local volunteer fire department's hoses had been cut and the telephone lines were downed added to this suspicion. In a twist of irony DuFran's Saloon was one of the few businesses to survive the conflagration.

As the Milwaukee Railroad continued construction the various towns along the route boomed and busted. LeBeau never recovered from the terrible fire of 1910 and is now submerged under the waters of Lake Oahe.

The Fighting Irishman from South Dakota

While Frank Leahy was born in Nebraska he was raised in Winner, South Dakota. There his high school football coach, Earl Walsh, gave him inspiration to play the game and to attend Notre Dame University. To gain admission Leahy was forced to attend an Omaha, Nebraska high school for his senior year.

Leahy played for the fighting Irish from 1927 until graduating in 1931. His college playing career, where he was listed as a 6 foot, 180 pound lineman, included the last three years of the coaching career of the legendary Knute Rockne. His playing days were followed by an immediate move into the coaching ranks, working as an assistant coach in Georgetown, Michigan State, and Fordham before becoming the head coach for Boston College in 1939. His two seasons at Boston rolled up an impressive 20 and 2 record, a win in the Orange Bowl and a National title. Then he returned home to Notre Dame.

His success with the Fighting Irish rivaled that of his old coach Knute. Despite taking two seasons off for military service he compiled an impressive record of 87 wins, 11 loses and 9 ties in 11 seasons. More impressive were the 6 undefeated seasons, 5 national titles, and an amazing 39 game winning streak in the late 1940's as well as the 1943 Heisman winner Angelo Bertelli.

Health concerns forced Frank Leahy to retire in 1954; he was selected for the National Football Foundation Hall of Fame in 1970. He died of heart failure in 1973 at the age of 65 in Oregon.

Much of Leahy's success might be attributed to his treatment of his players. He referred to them as 'his lads', lads that repaid him with a nearly 90% winning percentage as a head coach.

The Atomic Bomb from Canton

It is said that he watched in awe as the first atomic bomb launched its towering mushroom cloud into the New Mexico sky. If it were true Ernest Lawrence would have reason to be proud as well as awed. His work as a physicist and inventor paved the way for the atomic age.

Born in Canton, South Dakota in 1901, he showed his genius early. Even his high school teachers proclaimed him a prodigy and his higher education included degrees from the University of South Dakota, the University of Minnesota and Yale. By the age of 24 he was a National Research Fellow, and an associate professor by the time he was 27.

By 1930, now as a full professor at Berkley, he continued his work on the cyclotron, a device of his own invention that accelerates charged particles of atoms with electric impulses. It is a complicated device, you'd have to be a nuclear scientist to understand, but it is useful in creating artificial radioactivity. It also won Ernest Lawrence the Nobel Peace Prize for Physics in 1939.

By 1941 scientists of his caliber were all at work on the Manhattan project. Lawrence's laboratory was successful in producing the first Uranium 235, the materials of the first atomic bombs just a few years later. Bombs that Ernest Lawrence wanted detonated at sea as a demonstration to the Japanese military without harming civilians.

Shortly after his death in 1958, fellow scientists at Berkley discovered a new element, the 103 of the periodic table. They named it Lawrencium in honor of a South Dakota native who helped usher in the world of atomic power. More recently the National Research Laboratory at the University of California in Berkley has been named the Lawrence Science Lab.

A Guide and a Mom

She is one of the best-known women in American history. Her life and the life of her young son, Jean Baptiste, are chronicled as part of the Corps of Discovery 200 years ago. Unfortunately, it is only her years with the expedition that are well chronicled.

As we all know, Sacagawea came to the party of explorers when her husband, Toussaint Charbonneau, was hired to serve as a guide and interpreter. Actually, the young Shoshone woman served as an interpreter as well. Sacagawea spoke Shoshone and Hidatsa, her husband spoke Hidatsa and French, and another member of the party spoke French and English. Both Captains Lewis and Clark only spoke English.

Charbonneau and Sacagawea worked for the expedition for nearly 2 years. In August of 1806 they leave the expedition in present day South Dakota. The final tally for their services is $500 and 33 and a third cents. William Clark offers to take the child Jean Baptiste with him to raise and educate in St. Louis. The offer is declined; the nineteen-month-old child will not be weaned for another year.

The rest of Sacagawea's life is not well documented. We know that she gave birth to a daughter, Lisette, and most likely died at Fort Manuel Lisa in South Dakota at the young age of 25. Her children were adopted and raised by William Clark in St. Louis.

Sacagawea's accomplishments are many; guide, interpreter, and explorer would be just a partial list. You can add that she accomplished all these things while being first and foremost a mother.

Fannie and Nellie on the James

In the 1870's railroad mainlines had crossed the prairie on an east – west path serving communities like Aberdeen and Jamestown along the James River but between these communities there was no rail service in 1883. That year General M. R. Baldwin and Major James Peck formed the 'James River Navigation Company' on the northern part of the river.

The southern port of this riverboat line was Columbia, northeast of present day Aberdeen, South Dakota. The riverboats traveled north from there, going as far as Ypsilanti in North Dakota if the river was high. More commonly they traveled to LaMoure, Oakes or Port Emma, now known as Ludden, North Dakota.

The James River Navigation Company put two boats on the river, both in the neighborhood of 80 feet long and 20 feet wide at the beam. They named the side-wheeler the 'Nellie Baldwin' after the General's wife and the stern-wheeler the 'Fannie Peck' after the Major's wife and for three years these two gals prospered, moving freight and people along the James River. Not only were they utilized moving freight to the new settlements along the river; they also brought tourists and hunters north from the railroad terminal at Aberdeen.

But things deteriorated in 1886, the railroad laid tracks to Oakes, making the riverboats obsolete. Besides, dryer conditions that lowered the river level made steamer travel virtually impossible anyway.

The Fannie Peck was disassembled and shipped by rail to another river. The Nellie Baldwin was tied up at Columbia and never took to the river again. She fell into disrepair and deteriorated there.

Governor Bigelow of Vermillion

In March of 1861 the ink was barely dry on the proclamation forming the new Dakota Territory. Dr. William Jayne had been appointed by President Lincoln as the new Governor and charged with establishing a new government and choosing a site for its capital.

The cities of the territory, and there weren't more than a handful, all put on their best face when Governor Jayne toured the communities to select the capital.

A mounted messenger had brought word to the town of Vermillion that the Governor and his party were headed their way. We can only imagine the flurry of activity in that small community as the town fathers rode out to meet the distinguished gentlemen as they approached.

The occupants of the carriage were treated to a banquet of every imaginable food and speeches by the city fathers lauding the community's finest attributes. It must have come as quite a shock to those same city leaders when after two hours of festivities they were informed that the governor was now approaching the town.

The governor, accompanied by four carriage loads of lesser territorial officials, only stopped for a few moments in Vermillion before proceeding to Yankton and making it the seat of government for the new territory.

And the guests of honor at the Vermillion banquet? Well, G. B. Bigelow was greatly impressed by the community and of course surprised to be mistaken for the Governor. He thought this was how western towns greeted all new comers. He was so impressed that he decided to make his home in Vermillion, living out his life in that fine town that even occasionally referred to him as 'Governor Bigelow' in a case of mistaken identity.

A Gold Mine for the South Dakota Treasury

Some of the political discussions of the 1930's centered on the Gold Standard or the use of gold as money. While on the Gold Standard this country's money was either made of gold or, in the case of paper money, backed by gold deposits. That ended with a stroke of President Franklin Roosevelt's pen in 1933 when the private ownership of gold was outlawed with the exception of jewelry.

While such a move could be expected to depress or even bankrupt the gold mining companies of the Black Hills, the Gold Reserve Act, which went into effect in January of 1934, made them prosperous. The act required the federal government to buy the gold produced by the Homestake Mining Company, and other mines, for $35 per troy ounce. This guaranteed price and market generated a boom in the Deadwood and Lead vicinities of the Black Hills.

In 1934 the Homestake Company sold sixteen and a half million ounces of gold to Uncle Sam. And while stock values slumped for most business sectors the value of a share of Homestake Company increased from roughly $50 per share to nearly $450. Those stock values would continue to increase over the next years.

But it was not just the shareholders that benefited by the boom in gold prices. The 1935 South Dakota Legislature implemented a 4% gold ore tax. While the tax exempted all the small mines and in reality only applied to the Homestake Company it generated nearly three quarters of a million dollars in its first year. This was money that the state of South Dakota desperately needed to avoid insolvency during the depth of the depression. In fact, fully one third of the South Dakota government's revenues came from the depths of the Homestake Mine during the dark days of the great depression.

She Got the House in the Settlement.

For the Plains Indians who dwelt in earth lodges, most notably the Mandan, Hidatsa, and Arikara, building a new house was a major project. Lodges were generally thirty or more feet in diameter and would serve as a home to anywhere from ten to forty people.

First the floor was dug out to a depth of about a foot. Then posts were set along the edge of this floor, usually at a top height of about 5 feet with log beams connecting them. Closer to the center of the lodge 4 more posts were set at least 10 feet tall with beams again connecting the tops and forming a frame work for the lodge covering. Shorter logs would be used to run from the ground to the beams, these were covered first with branches or cattail rushes before being covered with dry grass and finally a foot layer of dirt and sod. The peak of the structure was left open for light to enter and for smoke to escape.

Timbers and sod also roofed the door. Openings were quite large to allow a man to enter without stooping while leading his horse. The floor plan was quite simple; the fire for heating and cooking was maintained in the center of the lodge, sacred objects were hung on the posts opposite the door, sleeping areas were arranged along the walls and the corral for the horses was near the door. The horses were only brought in during times of bad weather or during threat of attack.

All of this construction must have required hundreds or even thousands of hours of backbreaking effort all accomplished with stone or bone tools. Most notably it was almost entirely done by the women of the tribe, only with the lifting of the heavy crossbeams were the men allowed to help.

This had a practical implication in the society of the Earth Lodge dwelling Native Americans. It made the home the possession of the woman; if the marriage dissolved the wife got the house.

A Lady Doctor and Her Family

While woman doctors were in themselves a rarity back in the 19th century Dr. Abby Ann Jarvis was unique in many ways. She was the first woman in South Dakota who was both licensed as a pharmacist and as a physician. Quite an accomplishment given that she did not start her medical education until she was nearly 40 years old.

Born in Ohio in 1853 Abbie and her husband homesteaded near Faulkton, South Dakota in 1888. Her father was already a practicing physician in the area and Abby traveled with him as his assistant for four years before deciding she needed medical training herself. This was a monumental decision for the mother of five.

In the fall of 1892 she took her three daughters with her to Chicago where she enrolled as a student at the Woman's Medical College of Northwestern University. Her husband, now operating a drug store, stayed in Faulkton with the family's two sons. Jarvis's studies were delayed while she cared for her ill mother from 1895 to 1897. With her mother's death Abbie and her girls returned to Chicago and finished medical school in 1898.

Dr. Jarvis returned to Faulkton to continue her father's practice traveling in a buggy pulled by Ladybug. Her motto, which she had prominently displayed in her office, stated 'Prepare to respond to any call, day or night'. She continued to respond to the medical needs of the community until shortly before her death in 1931 at the age of 78. Dr. Abbie Ann Jarvis, a woman, mother, doctor, and pharmacist.

The Wizard of South Dakota

You might say that he was the Wizard of South Dakota before he was the Wizard of Oz. While his time in Aberdeen, South Dakota was relatively short it probably played a major role in his development as an author. L. Frank Baum was 32 years old when he came to the booming town of Aberdeen in 1888. Unfortunately, his arrival coincided with drought and a downturn in the local economy.

Baum's first enterprise in the hub city was as a storeowner. He operated what was referred to as a 'Fancy Goods' store named Baum's Bazaar. The store sold novelty and specialty items that were not available in the general stores of the day. The store was as well known for the stories told by its proprietor as it was for its inventory. As you would expect when times grew tough luxuries such as novelties were difficult to sell. This led Baum to try his hand at another endeavor in Aberdeen.

The 'Saturday Evening Pioneer' was a short-lived weekly newspaper known for it's coverage of social events. Baum himself wrote an often-satirical column called 'Our Landlady'. The paper fell to the same hard times as the store. In 1891 Baum commented that the sheriff wanted the paper more than he did and left Aberdeen for Chicago.

But of course he is best known for the book the 'Wizard of Oz' written in 1900. This book and its successors became some of the best loved children's books of the day and provided the basis for the classic movie in 1934.

Baum never enjoyed good health, suffering a heart attack while still in his 30's. He died on May 7, 1919 in Los Angeles, California at the age of 53.

L. Frank Baum's career, and by the way the L. stands for Lyman, is best known for his writings after he left our area. We like to think that his characters and stories were colored by his time in the Dakotas.

Put Another Cow Chip on the Fire

Keeping warm is a basic human necessity. A stove for heating and cooking was a required part of a pioneer cabin in the Dakotas, but what do you burn in that stove? If you lived where trees were plentiful the answer is as obvious as firewood. However, most of the Dakotas had too few trees to furnish the amounts of firewood needed by the early settlers.

There were some free sources of fuel. Cow chips are flammable, if they are dry enough and corncobs also will burn when dry. These commodities were free to the homesteaders of the Dakotas but might not be available in enough quantity to keep a tarpaper shack toasty all winter.

A number of other options were available depending on your location and funds. In the western part of what is now North Dakota lignite coal was a locally available commodity. Many settlers chose their land based on visible seams of lignite along creek banks or hills. For some the coal not only served as a source of heat in their home but also as a source of income, the coal sold to other settlers and to stores in town.

Certainly if the homesteader could afford it, purchased coal was the most common way to stay warm. Generally a wagonload would be piled beside the tarpaper shack and then dug out of the snow as needed through the winter.

But the Germans from Russia had their own, cheap and renewable source of fuel; they called it 'Mist'. Basically, 'Mist' is a combination of manure and straw, mixed together by walking horses or oxen through it. This was then formed into bricks and allowed to dry in the sun.

The Germans from Russia built many of their homes from sun dried clay bricks; they also kept themselves warm with sun dried manure bricks.

Herding on the Cheyenne Strip

In the very early years of the 1900's the cattle industry was booming on the short grass prairie of the northwestern part of South Dakota. The only difficulty these ranchers faced was access to railroad shipping. The nearest railroad tracks ended at Evarts just 90 miles away. Unfortunately those 90 miles had two major obstacles, Indian reservations and the Missouri River.

In 1902 the Milwaukee Railroad negotiated a lease of a narrow parcel of land from the Cheyenne River Reservation. The 6-mile wide, 87 mile long lease became known as 'The Strip' and was used as the trail from the west to the railheads along the Missouri. The herds were driven down the strip and crossed the Missouri on Pontoon bridges or on ferry boats before being loaded on rail cars for shipment to the eastern markets. The drive down 'the strip' could be expected to take most of a week.

The strip resulted in a boomtown at the railhead of Evarts. A town that fades away when the Missouri river is bridged at Mobridge in 1906.

The tribes were paid 25 cents per head for the cattle driven down the strip. Sheep were herded down the strip for free, possibly because many of the smaller ranches, some owned by Indians, raised sheep rather than cattle.

The fences and water holes of the strip were maintained by the Milwaukee Railroad and used by ranches big and small including the Matador Cattle Company and the Drag V owned by Murdo McKenzie, and the Shiedley Cattle Company managed by Ed Lemmon. Men who will lend their names to communities still in existence across the west river country today.

Take a Left at Washington.

The Montana gold rush came at an interesting time in American history. In the early 1860's the civil war was raging in the eastern part of the country. There was concern that the gold found in Alder Gulch and other diggings would find its way into the Confederate Treasury.

This prompted the Federal Government to organize wagon trains to take what they assumed would be good Union sympathizers to the diggings. Some of these trains were organized in Minnesota and traveled across the Dakota Territory.

In 1862 the United States Congress appropriated $5,000 for an overland wagon train on what was referred to as the northern route to Montana. The Minnesota Congressional delegation recommended James Fisk to lead the expedition. At the time of his appointment he was a Private in the Union Army serving in Tennessee. With his appointment he was commissioned as a Captain and returned to Minnesota to lead the westward trek.

The wagon train was organized at Fort Abercrombie, near present day Wahpeton, North Dakota, and proceeded north to near Pembina, then headed west, traveling along the United States - Canadian border. This route allowed them to avoid having to cross the Missouri River and also took them north of most of the traditional Indian hunting grounds.

James Fisk leads his wagon train across the prairie with little difficulty, and then according to his orders, he proceeded west to Walla Walla, Washington. There he sold the expedition's equipment, booked passage on a coastal freighter to Panama, hiked across the Isthmus, and then found another ship that brought him back to America.

Fisk and several of his officers managed to complete their round trip of North America in time to be back in Minnesota by February of 1863 to organize another trip westward. In fact Captain James Fisk makes this grueling journey a total of 4 times in the 1860's.

The Big Bang Theory

We all know that the Buffalo is a large animal; it should come as no surprise that the rifles that the buffalo hunter used were large weapons. While Remington, Ballard and probably some other manufacturers produced the heavy bore rifles that were the tools of the Buffalo Runner trade it was Christian Sharps who made the most notable rifle.

Many considered their 'Sharps Old Reliable' the epitome of the buffalo hunter's long-range gun. These were not light or cheap weapons. An 'Old Reliable' weighed as much as 12 or 13 pounds and would cost as much as $150 in the 1870's. Anyone setting out to make a living on the buffalo plains would have considered this an investment necessary for his success. The prices were said to plummet to as low as $25 or $30 after the end of the buffalo slaughter.

Just as today, guns were available in many calibers. A common buffalo hunting caliber was the 45-120-550. The bullet measured 45 hundredth of an inch, was propelled by black powder weighing 120 grains, and was made up of 550 grains of lead. This was the common way of describing cartridges in the Black Powder Cartridge era although quite often the weight of the bullet was dropped, shortening it to a 45-120 cartridge. These were reloadable in the field, making the hunter less reliant on supplies from town.

This method of describing firearms ended with the advent of smokeless powder. The different formulas available made uniform descriptions of powder weights obsolete. Most modern firearms are known only by their bore diameter and manufacturer, the lone commonly used throw back to the early days of cartridge firearms is the 30-30, originally a bore of 30 hundredth of an inch with a 30 grain black powder charge. An historic cartridge that many deer hunters of the Dakotas still use.

He Couldn't Take Home A Souvenir Spoon

During his 1843 trip up the Missouri River John James Audubon made a rather unique purchase. While at Fort Union he acquired from a local Indian woman a 5-month-old badger. This critter already had quite a few miles on it. It had been traded from tribe to tribe before ending up with Audubon and his party of naturalists. During their stay at Fort Union they kept the animal in the common room. Audubon considered the animal 'mischievous'; it generally tore up the place any time it was left alone.

Ultimately the badger had to be moved to another room where it could do less damage. It was fed twice a day, raw meat, given plenty of clean water and was considered clean in its habits. It also dug a hole under the fireplace hearth and tried to attack anyone who came near.

When Audubon returned east at the end of the summer he took the badger with him but not without difficulty. On the boat trip down the Missouri it gnawed its way out of his wooden cage. The badger was recaptured when one of the boat hands threw a buffalo robe over him and pinned him to the ground. He was returned to a newly reinforced enclosure.

Once they arrived in New York Audubon had a tin lined box filled with dirt as a new home for his 'pet'. The badger promptly dug a hole in which he spent most of his time.

Audubon studied this specimen for several months, commenting on changes in fur color and texture during the winter season. His painting of the badger for the book 'Quadrupeds of North America' pictures the animal in its natural prairie habitat, fiercely growling in defense of his territory. Territory that for this particular badger was thousands of miles away on the Dakota Plains.

Uff-da, I Have to Go to School

They say this country is the great melting pot, the place where people of all nationalities come to make a new life under one flag. But even 25 years into the 20th century, in many areas of the Dakotas, English was still a poorly spoken second language for many residents. Depending on the area and the ethnic group that had settled there Norwegian or German was much more likely to be heard on small town streets than English.

In the 1920's the Federal Government came up with a plan to change that. In selected communities, roughly a dozen in each Dakota, an Americanization Program was instituted. Any resident between the age of 16 and 25 who could not speak and read English at the fifth grade level was required to attend night school. At the time no one challenged the mandatory schooling for adults who could not pass a language proficiency test. In fact, some immigrant residents looked at the program as a way to prove their loyalty to this country. They would even wear buttons proclaiming the 'Americanization School' program.

The efforts of the Federal Government to make English the standard language of the land were probably the result of the post World War One patriotic fervor. These feelings were reinforced just a few years later when this country again faced war overseas.

The result here at home was that for many immigrants and their first generation American children, English became their town language, and at home among family they spoke what would be considered their native tongue.

The Devil's Dictionary

Ambrose Bierce and Samuel Clemens, better known as Mark Twain, both moved to San Francisco as they pursued their writing careers. While Samuel Clemens spent his early working days on the Mississippi River as a stern-wheeler pilot, Ambrose Bierce worked as a mining engineer. His greatest success occurred in the Black Hills. Under his direction the Black Hills Placer Mining Company dammed Spring Creek and diverted the water 17 miles by way of a flume bringing the water to Rockerville, a rich mining district that was too short of water for normal sluicing operations.

While the flume only operated for a few years it was considered one of the major engineering feats of the 1880's. But it was as an author that Ambrose Bierce made his biggest mark on the world. His wit and satirical commentary made him one of the most sought after authors of his day. His most notable work, considered the greatest satire of the 19th century, was the 'Devil's Dictionary'.

The dictionary gives us such definitions as a 'Hag', that's any elderly lady that you don't like and the four types of homicide; felonious, excusable, justifiable and praiseworthy. The definition continues to state that it probably didn't matter to the slain what category his death fell into but a classification system was handy for the lawyers.

Women and religion were common targets of the satirical pen of Ambrose Bierce. His dictionary referred to women as 'the unfair sex' and having a 'rudimentary susceptibility to domestication'. The 'Devil's Dictionary' referred to ministers as an 'agent of a higher power with lower responsibility' and saints as 'dead sinners, revised and edited'.

His views of politicians are probably still held by many. The 'Devil's Dictionary' definition of politics is 'conduct of public affairs for private advantage'. Even the highest office felt the wit of the Bierce pen, the presidency was defined as 'the greased pig of American politics'.

The book the 'Devil's Dictionary' was written in 1911 and while much of the satire now misses the mark, it is still in print.

Motor Cars and Laws

When the earliest cars arrived in the region in the first years of the 20th century they enjoyed nearly a dozen years with little or no regulation in North Dakota.

In 1911 the state instituted its first motor vehicle registration, licensing 7,140 cars and just 60 trucks. That's one vehicle for every eighty people living in North Dakota. Currently we are closer to a car or truck for each person in the state. Also in 1911 the state instituted its first speed limits for motorcars setting the top speed at 10 miles per hour in towns and at 30 miles per hour in the open country. The same law made a crime out of tampering with, operating, or driving a vehicle without the owner's consent. One law to cover speeding and Grand Theft Auto, now that's efficiency.

Fargo got its first police car in 1915, it makes you wonder how they enforced the speed limits without a car to catch the speeder during the previous four years.

And car horns were more useful in those early days of automobiles. Rather than turn signals, or even hand signals a code of horn toots could be used. One honk meant I am stopping, two blasts meant you stop I'm going ahead, and three toots meant look out, I'm backing up. It could get kind of loud if several cars were moving through an intersection at the same time.

All this made for more commotion than many of the horses of the day were prepared for. Most communities had laws forcing the car driver to slow when encountering horses on the road. Drivers were even required to stop and shut off the engine if the equine was spooking. Rules of the road that made the transition from a horse and buggy society to the day of the automobile a little more bearable.

Free Speech on the Prairie

Much of the Dakotas were settled by people of German ancestry, which made for some problems when the United States went to war against Germany. John H. Wishek was a successful businessman in early McIntosh County, in fact he was known as 'Father Wishek' in the area. Even though Wishek had been born in Pennsylvania, he was of German heritage and proud of it. In fact he was so proud of his past that he gave away a handful of copies of the booklet 'German Achievements in America' in the year of 1918.

Some business rivals lobbied for and secured Wishek's indictment under the 'Espionage Act' for distributing this Un-American literature. For three weeks the trial proceeded in Federal Court in Bismarck with the Honorable Charles Amidon presiding. During the trial Wishek's attorneys presented evidence that he had bought more liberty bonds than all of his accusers combined.

In the end Judge Amidon directed the jury that the prosecution witnesses held a private grudge against John Wishek. He also told the jury that the only things prohibited by the Espionage Act were interfering with the armed forces, inciting mutiny, or obstructing recruiting and unless the defendant intended to accomplish any of those acts by distributing his booklets he should be found not guilty.

Even with these instructions the jury is deadlocked with a 9 to 3 vote to acquit. While Wishek could have been retried on the charges he never was. He fared better than another victim of the anti-German fervor.

Reverend John Fontana was a naturalized American citizen serving as pastor to the German Evangelical Church in New Salem. Fontana did not believe in war, in fact he blamed President Wilson for the American involvement overseas. As a protest he refused to purchase liberty bonds, donate money to the Red Cross, or to display an American flag in his New Salem church.

He was charged under the Espionage Act and brought to trial before Judge Amidon in Bismarck. Despite Judge Amidon's instructions to the jury that none of these actions were crimes the jury convicts Reverend Fontana who is sentenced to three years in the penitentiary.

While the conviction will be overturned on appeal, that will take time. During the appeal process the church at New Salem refuses to dismiss Reverend Fontana, listing him as the pastor despite his incarceration. Later the German Evangelical Church chooses him as the featured speaker at the dedication of the new church in Hebron.

Judge Amidon presided over several such trials in North Dakota; in each case he interpreted the law as prohibiting acts against the military, not merely unpatriotic speech giving the state a reputation as an 'oasis of sanity in a desert of hysteria'.

Grigsby's Roughriders

We all know the story of Theodore Roosevelt's part in the Spanish American War. How he formed a regiment of cowboys and socialites that became the Roughriders and charged to fame up San Juan Hill.

But there was another unit that also bore the nickname 'Roughriders'. The 3rd US Volunteer Cavalry was formed by the Attorney General of South Dakota, Melvin Grigsby. Five of the regiments twelve companies were raised in South Dakota with Montana, North Dakota and Nebraska contributing the other seven units. They came to be known as Grigsby's Roughriders.

One of the most common occupations listed by the South Dakota recruits was 'cowboy'. Francis Huston of Company A not only gave his occupation as cowboy on his enlistment papers but under hometown wrote 'on the range'. Company A's Captain, Seth Bullock, an early lawman in the Black Hills, listed his occupation as 'stockman' at the time of enlistment.

Grigsby's Roughriders don't get the glory that goes to Teddy and his regiment. In fact they do not leave the country. The unit was stationed at Camp Thomas at Chickamauga, Georgia for training. The Spanish American War ended before they could be deployed to Cuba.

Even though Grigsby's Roughriders never saw combat it did suffer casualties. Conditions at the overcrowded Camp Thomas were less than healthy. Nine members of the 3rd died of disease while stationed there and 22 were discharged due to ill health. Typhoid and other diseases were so common at Camp Thomas that Private William Hagler, originally detailed as the regimental veterinarian was reassigned to the post hospital as a nurse on August 1st.

The troopers of the 3rd were mustered out of service on September 8, 1898, just 4 months after they enlisted in Grigsby's Roughriders.

A Walking Stick by Any Other Name

Take about a six-foot long wooden shaft, top it with a double edged spear point, mount a metal cross bar a few inches below the point and a metal cap on the other end of the shaft and you have an espontoon.

During the revolutionary war era it was considered a badge of authority for infantry officers. It could be used to signal troops by waving it overhead and it could also be used by the officer as a last line of defense in battle. It had been used since the days of the Knights of the Roundtable, referred to as a halberd, half pike, or spontoon at various times in history.

Captain Lewis carried one with him during the entire three-year expedition, carrying the espontoon in one hand and his rifle in the other as he walked along the shoreline. The espontoon served him as a rifle rest, walking stick and in some cases a weapon.

The journals of the expedition make three references to the espontoon saving the day. Lewis killed a rattlesnake with his in May of 1805, later that month Clark killed a wolf at close range with his half pike.

But the most dangerous encounter came near Great Falls, Montana. A grizzly bear stalked and charged Captain Lewis who was caught with an unloaded rifle. With the bear in hot pursuit Lewis took refuge in the river, hoping to draw the bear into deep water and then use the espontoon to defend himself.

The bear evidently had his good shoes on; he broke off pursuit at the river's edge leaving Captain Lewis pondering the lesson of always reloading your rifle.

Camel Feed for the Dakotas

Born in Denmark and educated in Iowa, Niels Ebbison Hansen made his greatest contribution on the plains of the Dakotas. For years farmers had faced difficulties in finding crops; especially forage crops, that were hearty enough for the harsh climate they faced.

While working as the head of South Dakota State College's agriculture experiment station, Hansen took on the challenge of finding new crops, trees, and other plants that would thrive. He took the search overseas, traveling to Russia and China eight times between 1897 and 1934.

His greatest finds came in an area of Russia that had as extreme a climate as you find in the Dakotas. Summer temperatures rose to as high as 115 degrees and winter lows would drop to as cold 50 degrees below. The area even had as little rain as the western Dakotas.

From this area in Siberia new varieties of fruit trees and grasses such as Crested Wheatgrass and Brome grass were imported to the Dakotas providing gardeners and farmers with new crops.

And on one of these trips he noticed a couple of camels eating some hay, not grass hay but alfalfa, he brought back seeds from both the blue and yellow flowered alfalfa and crossed them to yield what he referred to as 'Cossack Alfalfa'. A forage crop that soon covered much of the Northern Plains.

While Hansen had many interests, he routinely published poetry, read voraciously, and even helped compose the South Dakota State College School song, horticulture remained his first love. His work can still be found in seed catalogs, including the Gurney Seed Company,

For his efforts Niels Hansen was known as the 'Burbank of the Plains' and every time you drive past an alfalfa field you are driving past his efforts.

The Blood Thirsty Hoards of Fort Union

Bed bugs were a common problem in many of the homes of the 1800's. The one-fifth inch long insect made its home in bedding and furniture, coming out at night to bite and draw blood from its victims. Kerosene and turpentine used in washing walls and bedding seemed to be the common remedies to a bed bug problem, but sometimes, such as this case at Fort Union, the bugs got the upper hand.

It seems in one of the local boarding houses at the fort the bed bug population had become a bit troublesome. According to a newspaper article published in 1865, 'it was best to go to bed with a candle in one hand and a revolver in the other', to defend yourself against the bloodthirsty insects.

Not only were the little bugs hungry they were organized too, the article stated that the insects had organized into divisions and army corps complete with officers and soldier bugs. And while research tells us that the standard bed bug is one-fifth of an inch long, at Fort Union they came in all sizes, from 4 fitting on the head of a pin to a single bug being roughly the size of a mud turtle.

The satirical article went on to say that you had to be careful when dealing with the bed bugs of Fort Union because they were not content to suck a little blood; they were planning on carrying off the whole person.

Bed bugs ceased to be a problem by the mid 1940's. DDT proved to be an effective fumigant and became readily available after World War II, just about 80 years too late to help those needing a little unmolested sleep at Fort Union.

The Elk's Suspenders

During his trip up the Missouri River in 1843 John James Audubon and his party made a point of studying as closely as possible the animals of the west. In many cases they accomplished this by hunting the animal and studying the carcass.

But in the case of the elk they encountered some difficulties. During the entire summer they only had one shot at an elk and that was wasted by a misfiring muzzleloader. But they did have one chance at capturing a fawn.

While the party was headed up stream on board the 'Omega', they stopped to load firewood. There they happened upon an elk fawn along the river where the bank was too steep for it to head inland away from the river. Alexis Labombarde, a servant of Pierre Chardon the fur trader hosting the Audubon trip, was sent to capture the little spotted elk fawn. Due to the steep banks Alexis was able to get hold of the young animal.

That's when things started to get difficult. Alexis didn't have a rope to tie the fawn so instead stripped his suspenders and trussed up the fawn with them. Despite help from others on the boat, none of which had brought a rope, the fawn slipped out of his makeshift lasso and escaped into the Missouri River and swam away to freedom.

The painting of the elk in the book 'Quadrupeds of North America' was based on two elk that John James Audubon purchased from a farmer in Pennsylvania who had raised them. They stood in for the elk of the prairie that had eluded them all summer.

Vote Early, Vote Often

The Minnesota Territory originally included not only the area we know as Minnesota but what is now known as North and South Dakota and the eastern portions of what is known Wyoming and Montana. However, when Minnesota achieved statehood in 1858 the western portions of the original Minnesota Territory were left unorganized.

While this will be remedied in 1861 with the formation of the Dakota Territory for three years there was no government in that area. This did not stop people from trying to gain representation in Congress. In 1859 an election was held for a delegate to the United States Congress from 'the area part of the Territory of Minnesota but not part of the state of Minnesota, now known by common consent as Dakota'.

Jefferson Kidder won the race with nearly 1700 votes over his challenger Alpheus Fuller who received just 147 votes. Quite a landslide for Kidder, who was a lawyer involved with land deals through the Dakota Land Company, and a resident of St. Paul, Minnesota.

However, Kidder was not seated by the United States Congress. It was not that he was representing a territory that was not officially organized by the United States. The problem dealt with the number of votes that had been cast.

The best estimate of the population of the area known by common consent as Dakota put the number of voters, white males over the age of 21, at roughly fifty people. They each would have had to have voted nearly forty times to account for the tally reached in that first election.

Kidder will win a seat as the delegate from the Dakota Territory in the United States Congress in the election of 1874 and is reelected in 1876. During his time in Washington he is a vocal advocate for the opening of the Black Hills of South Dakota to white settlement. At the direction of President Grant he introduces an amendment that authorizes a commission and funding to end the treaty giving the Sioux title to the area.

Let's Build Us a New Elevator

Farmers all across the Midwest have long believed that the prices they receive for their wheat and other crops are too low and subject to excessive speculation. In the early 1900's the voters of North Dakota decided to do something about that.

In 1912 a state constitutional amendment authorizing the construction of state owned grain terminals outside North Dakota passed by a 3 to 1 margin. Every county but McIntosh voted in favor of the issue. While the Non-Partisan League that had sponsored the amendment waited for construction to begin state officials balked, stating that without state owned terminals and elevators within North Dakota the venture would fail.

This prompted another amendment to be placed on the general election ballot in 1914. This time the measure authorized the construction of state owned grain terminals both within North Dakota and outside the state. Again the issue passed by a three to one margin and again McIntosh County was the only county opposing. It is assumed the heavy Germans from Russia population was too conservative for this type of endeavor.

Now with two landslide victories the Non-Partisan League felt assured that the North Dakota landscape would soon bristle with state owned grain handling facilities shipping the state's farm production to grain terminals for export and processing. This obviously didn't happen, the State Board of Control, the agency responsible for government buildings, lobbied the legislature not to construct the farmer-envisioned network of grain terminals claiming they were unnecessary. The 1915 legislature repealed the tax despite protests from the farmers of the state.

While the farmers had succeeded at the ballot box they had failed at the state capital. This prompted the Non-Partisan League to be more aggressive in backing and electing candidates for state office. After the 1916 election League members held roughly 80% of the state House and the governor's mansion.

A Colorful Foreigner

They say we are a nation of immigrants, and that also applies to our region's most prestigious game bird. The first pheasants to make the trip across the Pacific from China were released in Oregon in 1880. The American Ambassador to Shanghai, O. N. Denny shipped 70 birds to his brother who released them in the Willamette Valley where they thrived and became the breeding stock for propagation programs around the country.

By 1891 South Dakotans were discussing and maybe even importing these Chinese fowl themselves. However, the first documented releases of pheasants in the state came in 1898 when Dr. Arne Zetlitz of Sioux Falls purchased several birds. He kept this breeding stock in captivity, releasing the young hatches in Minnehaha county over the next years. The young pheasants thrived on the South Dakota prairies and by 1902 could be found as far away as Yankton.

During the first decade of the 20th Century many individuals and civic groups around the state continued the importation and propagation of these colorful foreign birds. The first state sponsored releases came in 1911 when 48 pairs of pheasants were freed in Spink County.

Despite what appears to be a haphazard attempt at introducing this new alien species to the prairie environment the pheasant thrived. The first South Dakota hunting season for the Chinese Ringneck Pheasant came in 1919. By the late 1930's average hunting bags swelled to over a million and half birds a year, making the pheasant a major factor in the South Dakota economy.

Crawling the Walls at Fort Mandan

On February 9, 1805 Private Thomas Howard made an error in judgment. The private returned to Fort Mandan after dark and rather than hale the sentry and be admitted through the gate he scaled the cottonwood logs that made up the fort wall.

Unfortunately, his illicit entry into the fort was witnessed by at least two individuals. The sentry who reported the act to the Captains and by a Mandan Indian who followed Private Howard over the wall. The Corps of Discovery was concerned that tribes other than the Mandan, who were considered friendly, would realize how vulnerable the small fort and its garrison was to attack.

Captain Lewis first dealt with the Indian. He had the young warrior brought to him and explained to him that he had come very close to being shot as an intruder. After a lecture that put more than a little fear into the Mandan, Captain Lewis sent him on his way with a small gift of tobacco.

The journals kept by the Captains do not indicate why Private Howard was out and about on this cold February evening. Most likely he was out hunting or performing some other duty of the expedition. Certainly if he had been out on what could be considered a social visit it would have been noted in the legal proceedings that followed.

In fact, that very morning a court-martial was convened. Private Howard was charged with 'setting a pernicious example to the savages'. A crime of which he was found guilty and sentenced to fifty lashes on the back.

Perhaps because of his long, excellent record as a soldier, perhaps because his offense was an error of judgment the same court that found him guilty and set his sentence also recommended leniency. Capitan Lewis concurred and suspended the sentence. This would prove to be the last court-martial of the Corps of Discovery.

Let's Count the Cash

The story broke on January 8, 1895; South Dakota Treasurer William Walter Taylor had fled to South America and taken nearly $367,000 of the state's money with him. Taylor was a former banker from Redfield and was retiring from the position of state treasurer. His theft and flight from the country took everyone by surprise.

Taylor's South American holiday was short lived, he returned voluntarily to South Dakota within a few months and was convicted and sentenced to 20 years in prison. This sentence was reduced to 2 years on appeal, which he served before his release. Between the money returned by Taylor, his own wealth that was seized, and his bonds, including the personal wealth of former Governor Mellette, the state's taxpayers only came up short about $100,000.

This scandal obviously had an impact on the next statewide elections. In 1896 the Democrats supported Populist candidate Andrew Lee for governor. Lee, a native of Norway, won a landslide victory. Given the recent events the public and Governor Lee had little faith in how the state was being run. One of his first official acts was to order all of South Dakota's bank deposits be withdrawn and brought to Pierre in cash to be counted.

Armed guards, South Dakota National Guard troops, and even regular Army soldiers brought bags totaling $257,482.71 to the legislative hall to be counted.

Problems occur when the money is returned to the Chicago banks. A blizzard stranded the train carrying $190,000 of the taxpayer's money near Highmore, South Dakota. A rescue train from Huron was also stranded near Wolsey, South Dakota. Authorities worried that if the train had been robbed the State of South Dakota would have been bankrupt. Fortunately, all the money was safely returned to the banks leaving South Dakota solvent.

The South Dakota Courtesy Patrol

In 1935 Governor Tom Berry decided that the state of South Dakota needed to not only enforce its new traffic laws but also educate the public and provide assistance to stranded motorists. Ten officers were selected for the newly formed 'Courtesy Patrol'. These officers were charged with patrolling the highways and gravel roads of the state not only looking for speeders and other traffic violators but lending assistance to any marooned travelers they might encounter.

Each officer was issued a towrope, a gallon can of gasoline, a first aid kit and orders to not leave any stranded traveler until they were back on their way. Even with automobile travel curtailed due to the depression it still was a daunting job for the ten officers of the patrol. Each worked twelve-hour shifts, seven days a week and was considered 'on call' the rest of the time.

Two way radios weren't available in the mid 1930's, the courtesy patrol officers stopped at filling stations along their patrols, checking with headquarters for any accidents or stranded travelers in the area.

The 'Courtesy Patrol' lasts just two years. In 1937 the South Dakota Department of Justice was disbanded and the task of enforcing the rules of the road fell to the Highway Department. They formed a new unit called the 'Motor Patrol' with eight men headed by the former Aberdeen Police Chief Walter Goetz.

The motor patrol shared one trait with its predecessor the 'courtesy patrol'. They didn't get two-way radios until 1948; by that time the unit numbered forty officers and would become the South Dakota Highway Patrol that we know today.

Death of a Legend

We hardly know any more about the death of Sacagawea than we know about her life. On December 20, 1812, just 6 years after the return of the Corps of Discovery the 25-year-old woman dies of putrid fever at Fort Manuel in present day South Dakota. Her passing noted by the Missouri Fur Company clerk John Luttig.

While Luttig mentions that Sacagawea leaves a fine infant daughter he does not mention when the child, Lisette, was born. Some modern medical doctors assume that the 'Putrid Fever' was actually a post partum infection. This may have been complicated by Pelvic Inflammatory Disease possibly brought on by gonorrhea. These speculations based on a number of mentions in the Lewis and Clark journals regarding Sacagawea's health as well as other journals of the time.

Little is known about Sacagawea's life after the Lewis and Clark expedition. We assume that most of the time was spent along the Missouri River where her husband could work as a trader. We do know that in 1809 Sacagawea, her husband, and her son Jean Baptiste journeyed to St. Louis. There Jean Baptiste, or Pomp, as he had been known on the Corps of Discovery expedition was left with Captain Clark who had volunteered to see to his education. Captain Clark later took on the responsibility of raising Lisette as well, adopting the girl the year after her mother's death.

While we know much about Jean Baptiste's life, including his tour of Europe with royalty, no official record of Lisette exists after her adoption by Captain Clark in 1813.

Sacagawea was buried near Fort Manuel; the gravesite has never been discovered and may now be under the waters of Lake Oahe but monuments to the young women have been erected all across the United States, including, the most recent dollar coin.

By God, We Need a Motto

As the Dakota Territory prepared for statehood various conventions and committees were convened to prepare a constitution and the other official trappings of statehood. Even things as mundane as a motto required a great deal of thought and consideration. When governments need to think hard they form a committee.

The motto committee for the proposed state of South Dakota was formed in 1885, a full 4 years before statehood. At its head was Dr. Joseph Ward, an esteemed early minister in Yankton and the founder of Yankton College. He and his fellow committee members settled on this phrase 'By God the People Rule'.

But it was printer Sam Clover who read it and became concerned, he felt that the phrase could be interpreted as blasphemous, as in 'By God!!! The people rule'. Even though Clover had been working late into the night when he came upon this revelation he felt it important enough to wake the sleeping Reverend Ward.

The good reverend sleepily saw the possibility of misinterpretation and substituted the word 'under' for the word 'by'. Giving us the official State Motto for South Dakota that is still in use today 'Under God the People Rule'.

If it hadn't been for a sharp-eyed printer on the lookout for blasphemy in any form South Dakota might have a slightly different motto and 'by God' that's another Great Story of the Great Plains.

Give Me a Beer

The state constitutions of both North and South Dakota prohibited alcohol manufacture and sale within the states. Those state prohibition laws had been replaced by national prohibition in 1919 with the ratification of the 18th amendment. For 14 years bootleggers, smugglers, and moonshiners provided alcohol, illegally of course, around the country.

That changes in the 1930's with consideration of the 21st amendment. On December 5, 1933 Utah became the 36th state to ratify the constitutional amendment repealing prohibition and legally allowing alcohol sale across the land. But South Dakota was well ahead of the game. Governor Berry had called a special legislative session during the previous summer legalizing the manufacture and sale of beer in South Dakota.

The law had no effect while alcohol remained constitutionally prohibited but when the 21st amendment was ratified South Dakota became one of the first states to have not only state laws allowing the manufacture and sale of booze but more importantly tax it.

This gave the cash strapped state a source of revenue needed to match the Federal funds available for relief programs under the Federal Emergency Relief Agency.

For South Dakotans battling drought and depression it gave them a chance to wash away the dust with a cold brew, with the tax on that bottle of beer funding some of the New Deal relief programs across the state.

Charging for Cheap Land

There was a great debate in the late 1880's regarding the land in the Sisseton – Wahpeton Reservation. As the residents of that reservation moved towards farming they required less land than during their more nomadic days. The government had been in negotiation with Chief Renville and other members of his tribe for nearly a decade regarding compensation to the Indians for the excess land.

Chief Renville and Territorial Governor Mellette traveled to Washington, DC to seek a plan to open the excess land to settlers. The tribe had claimed large blocks of land, in addition each man, woman, and child of the tribe was allocated a quarter section of their own. This left nearly 600,000 acres of land available to the public.

At noon, April 15, 1892 the land was opened to settlers. Officers and troops from nearby Fort Sisseton patrolled the border, turning back sooners and signaling the start of the rush at noon. At towns all along the border hundreds of land hungry people awaited the sound of the bugle or carbine shot that would signal high noon and the start of the rush.

At Waubay, South Dakota, an estimated 500 homesteaders awaited the signal, nearly 1000 charged from Brown's Valley and 500 started their trek from the town of Travare, South Dakota. At Wheaton, South Dakota the only path to the cheap land crossed a privately owned toll bridge. The owner of the bridge tried to control traffic and collect his fee, but nearly 600 people overwhelmed him and crossed without paying the toll.

But the most interesting part of the land rush came along the new Milwaukee Railroad line. The train crossed the line at precisely noon proceeding to the end of the track two miles into the new territory. There, land seekers were able to buy horses to rush to the prime pieces of land.

Those horses sold to them by enterprising Indians who were the only people allowed on the reservation before noon. The Indian monopoly on horseflesh allowed them to garner a premium price for whatever ponies they chose to sell. Enough settlers purchased the Indian ponies and rushed ahead to found the city of Sisseton in just a matter of minutes.

Stagecoaches, Fires and Curses

It was during the fall of 1871 that stagecoaches started to run between Fort Abercrombie, near present day Wahpeton, North Dakota, and Pembina along the United States Canadian border. The four horse coaches made the trips three times per week along the east or Minnesota side of the river.

Riverboat traffic had started years earlier but was seasonal at best. The stagecoaches could be considered a more reliable but more dangerous method of moving along the frontier.

The stage stations along the route, usually crude log shelters with sod roofs and dirt floors, fostered new communities including Georgetown now known as Moorhead, Minnesota. Other stage stops, like Elm River and Kelley's Point have been lost to history. At these stops horse teams would be changed and meals served. Salt pork and beans, the usual bill of fare, cost 50 cents a plate. You could also bed down for the night at these stations, sleeping on the dirt floors for the same cost.

While Indians would not have been a major source of fear in the eastern Dakotas and Minnesota in 1871 there were other dangers. One stagecoach encountered a prairie fire burning across its path. The winds were driving the flames towards the coach road making turning back dangerous. This left stagecoach driver 'Limpy Jack Clayton' with one option, an end run around the conflagration.

For the passengers it must have been a wild and smoky ride bouncing across the open prairie. Despite the flames, smoke and jarring ride the most notable part of the experience for the passengers was the vocabulary of the driver.

It seems that Limpy Jack Clayton could be quite creative, colorful and profane when encouraging his team of horses to pull a little harder and faster.

A Rock by Any Other Name

Lewis and Clark were the first white men to notice the rock. They noted in their Journal the odd shaped stone and while they did not give a name to the rock, they did name the nearby creek 'Stone Idol Creek' in honor of the stone.

For whatever reason the Federal Government renamed the rock in 1873, assigning it the name Standing Rock. Five years later the newly formed reservation in the area would be named it.

As is almost always the case, the Native American who lived in the area knew it most intimately. They had named the rock centuries earlier; they even had a legend about how the stone came to be.

It seems that a young girl was being punished for telling her parents a lie; she basically was grounded in the tipi. Late that night the crying girl snuck out, her parents thought that she was going out to talk to the spirits alone so they did not pursue the child. When she had not returned the next morning they began to look around. Instead of a young lady they found a new odd shaped rock on a butte to the north of the camp. Since the girl never returned it was believed that the spirits had turned the girl into stone for her misdeeds. The Sioux considered the 'Sitting Woman Rock' Sacred. While other tribes in the region had other legends regarding Standing Rock this tale would certainly be useful when lecturing a youth on truthfulness.

Whatever name you assign it, Stone Idol, Sitting Woman, or Standing Rock it was moved to Fort Yates and now stands outside the Agency Headquarters for the Standing Rock Reservation. A move that was accompanied by ceremonies attended by Indian Agent James McLaughlin and by Sioux Medicine Man Sitting Bull.

Up, Up and Away

In the 1930's helium balloons accomplished the exploration of high altitudes, not planes or rockets. The exploration of the stratosphere was a joint project of the United States Army Air Corp and the National Geographic Society. They chose as the center of these explorations what became known as the Stratosphere Bowl in the South Dakota Black Hills. The unique crater was chosen because the rock walls sheltered the balloon from winds while it was being filled.

In July of 1934 Explorer One was launched amid national press coverage. At an altitude of about 12 miles the balloon tore and crashed near Holdredge, Nebraska. The project's two-man crew managed to parachute to safety.

A second attempt to explore the stratosphere didn't even get off the ground when the balloon split just an hour before takeoff.

But on November 10, 1935 Explorer Two made history. Captains Orvil Anderson and Albert Stevens of the Army Air Corps, wearing the leather football helmets of the day, climbed into the gondola below the 300-foot balloon to start what would become a record setting flight. Before the end of their 8-hour voyage they climb above 72,000 feet, nearly 14 miles above the surface of the earth for a new altitude record.

During the flight Anderson and Stevens made scientific observations while floating through the stratosphere high above the plains of Western South Dakota before landing near White Lake, South Dakota. They also tested radio equipment; from their high vantage they were able to reach both Europe and Asia with the Shortwave Radio on board.

It was the last flight of the Stratosphere Program from the Black Hills but for the rest of the 1930's a little crater near Rockerville, South Dakota was home to the highest-flying men in the world.

The Gang that Couldn't Ride Straight

Long before Harry Longabaugh, better known as the Sundance Kid, met up with Robert Leroy Parker, better known as Butch Cassidy, he traveled the outlaw trail with the Curry gang. While the gang's first heist, in Idaho in 1896, netted them nearly $10,000, their second attempt didn't go nearly as well.

On June 28, 1897 the Curry Gang hit the Butte County Bank in Belle Fourche, South Dakota. From the start it didn't seem to go well, witnesses state that once the gang had everyone disarmed and with their hands in the air they didn't seem to know what to do next. About this time a passing shopkeeper noticed the commotion through a window and raised the alarm. The gang exited quickly with just $97 from the cash drawer for their efforts.

But if the robbery went badly the escape was a complete disaster. Gang member Tom O'Day lost control of his horse as he tried to mount. The only other mount at the hitching post was a mule that O'Day appropriated. Unfortunately, this was an extremely barn sour animal that headed towards its home, the opposite direction that the gang was fleeing town. The hapless criminal finally bailed off the mule and hid out in an outhouse on the edge of Belle Fourche. Tom O'Day was captured immediately.

Now that they had a prisoner the citizens of Belle Fourche had to figure out what to do with him. The city jail had burned down just days previously leaving only the steel barred cage of the cell standing. This sufficed as an open air holding cell until the locals starting talking about lynching the hapless outlaw. Law enforcement officials moved O'Day to the most secure spot in town; they held him in the very bank vault he had tried to rob earlier before moving him to better facilities in Deadwood.

The rest of gang tried to flee town while one of the local town's people unlimbered his rifle to take a shot at the fleeing outlaws. His shot dropped the horse from under the local blacksmith who was leading the first attempt at pursuit. Despite the rough start a posse was organized and pursued the rest of the gang until they were captured near Red Lodge, Montana and returned to jail in Deadwood from which they promptly escaped on Halloween night of 1897.

I'm the Governor, But of What?

In the 1850's what is now the eastern part of the Dakotas was a part of the Minnesota Territory but when Minnesota became a state in 1858 its boundaries did not include what we now know as the eastern part of North and South Dakota.

Many of the political leaders who were left just a little bit west of Minnesota assumed that a new territory would be organized quickly. They were so sure that a new Dakota Territory would be formed that they just went ahead and elected a governor for it and sent a representative off to Washington.

In 1858 the County Commissioners of Big Sioux County elected a territorial legislature, which then elected Henry Masters as Governor, James Allen as Secretary of State and sent Alpheus Fuller to Washington as a delegate to congress. Fuller was denied a seat by the full house.

With this newly formed government basically ignored by the Feds the political leaders went back to the drawing board. In 1859 they held another election. Jefferson Kidder was named as a delegate to Congress and Wilmot Brookings was elected governor. Again the powers in Washington ignored the new, unofficial, Dakota Territory.

Through all of this preterritorial political maneuvering the unofficial capital of the unofficial territory was Sioux Falls. The political leaders were all associated with the Dakota Land Company and members of the Democratic Party. But with the election of 1861 the Republicans were in control.

With the start of the Lincoln administration in 1861 the Dakota Territory is officially recognized and sent its first Governor, William Jayne. One of his first acts is to establish Yankton as the Territorial Capital. If you read the history books Dr. Jayne is credited as the first Governor of the Dakota Territory. A claim that Mr. Masters and Mr. Brookings might dispute.

Early Team Sports on the Prairie

The Corps of Discovery had seen the gigantic track and heard the stories from the Indians about the great bears. It was described as huge, ferocious and hard to kill. The first encounter with the grizzly for the members of the Lewis and Clark expedition came on October 20, 1804 near present day Mandan, North Dakota.

Private Cruzatte, better known for being the corps' near sighted fiddle player, was the first to encounter what the Americans of the day referred to as the White Bear. Cruzatte only wounds the bear and is forced to abandon his rifle and tomahawk as he flees the wounded bruin. Cruzatte's nearsightedness and poor marksmanship will continue through the expedition, on the return trip he mistakes Captain Lewis for an elk, wounding him in the 'back of the upper thigh'.

It is not until the next spring that the Corps of Discovery actually bags a grizzly. Even after 5 rifle balls fired into its heart and lungs and numerous shots into other parts of its body the bear swims the Missouri and hides in the brush for twenty minutes before dying. By May 13, 1805 Captain Lewis states in his journal that 'the curiosity of the crew is pretty well satisfied in regard to these animals'.

Grizzly bears continued to be a fixture on the plains well after the Lewis and Clark expedition. An 1865 newspaper, the 'Frontier Scout' of Fort Union, included an article about the hunting in what is now the Williston, North Dakota, area. They noted that deer, elk, and buffalo were plentiful, and while the buffalo were easy to shoot they were hard to kill. They also noted that while a number of grizzly bears had been encountered the hunters had always been alone and did not try a shot.

Evidently in the days of muzzle loading, single shot rifles, hunting grizzly bears was a team sport.

They Hang Horse Thieves

Crime and punishment on the frontier of the badlands in the western part of what is now North Dakota was sometimes an individual, not government, function.

Theodore Roosevelt related an incident in his book 'Ranch Life and the Hunting Trail' about a woman who felt justice should be swift and brutal, and color blind. For a woman living alone, she had run her husband off the ranch earlier that year, protecting her property and even the property of her guests could be a challenge.

You see the lady, whom Teddy doesn't name, was known through out the area for the fine buckskin hunting shirts, leggings, and gauntlets that she produced. This had drawn the future president to her cabin to place an order for a new hunting shirt. When he arrived he noticed three Indians who had stopped to trade deerskins for food with the woman and heard this story.

Shortly after the Sioux had arrived, a traveler, probably on the trail from Deadwood, had tried to steal their horses. The Indians had managed to thwart this theft and capture the horse thief but then arose the question of what to do with him. The lady buckskin maker suggested an immediate hanging, promising the Indians that she wouldn't ever 'cheep about it'. One Bull and his friends took a less drastic course of action, taking his gun and sending him on his way.

Roosevelt felt the woman's sense of justice admirable. He states that he wished he could make her the Sheriff or Indian Agent. She made all who came to her ranch, be they White or Red, toe the line.

While we have no definitive information we do not believe that this pioneer woman from the western Dakota Prairies was offered a position in the Roosevelt administration fifteen years later.

The 'South Dakota Today'

He is a rags to riches story that you might read about in one of his newspapers. Allen Neuharth was born and raised in Eureka, South Dakota. Even in high school he had aspirations of working in the newspaper industry in his home state. But it was after he left the state that he had his greatest successes.

Neuharth's first attempt as a publisher was less than a shining success. In 1952 he and a partner began a weekly sports paper in Rapid City. 'Sodak Sports' lasted just two years, folding in 1954 after losing nearly $50,000. Neuharth was devastated and tried to put the experience far behind him.

This led him to a series of jobs all across the nation. Positions with papers in Florida, Michigan and New York were part of a rise through the management ranks that ultimately led to the position of Chairman of Gannett Company, the largest newspaper company in the nation at the time.

But Neuharth's biggest success came in 1984 when he founded 'USA Today' the only national daily paper. The paper was established on the premise of highlighting the good news of the day. The paper is also known for the development of the colorful graphics that have become common in many of today's papers. In fact, Neuharth referred to his new paper's style as 'television on paper'.

Allen Neuharth took an early goal of being a newspaper reporter in South Dakota and turned it into a success that is recognized throughout the country. He has authored a number of books and a communications library bears his name at the University of Florida.

A Steam Belching, Water Walking, Dragon

After the War of 1812, or as it was known by most Americans at the time, the Second War for Independence, the army saw the need for western forts. Discussions around the war department concerned a line of posts along one of the western rivers.

In 1819 plans were made to place a line of army posts along the Missouri from its mouth at St. Louis north to the Mandan Villages. The army even ordered a new steamboat to serve as transportation for the planned expansion. The 'Western Engineer' was a 75-foot long sternwheeler that drew just 19 inches of water. It also had a carved figurehead of a dragon on the bow, and to make the boat more awe inspiring to the natives, boat builders vented the 'Western Engineer's' whistle through the mouth of the carving. Basically, whenever the captain blew the whistle the dragon snorted steam.

We'll never know what the plains Indians would have thought about the steam belching ship. The 'Western Engineer' spent the winter of 1819 at Council Bluffs, Iowa. That winter Congress revoked the appropriations for the Missouri River outposts when tax revenues shrank following the economic panic of 1819. Evidently in the early 1800's the Federal Government didn't spend money that it didn't have.

For nearly forty more years the transportation and commerce on the Missouri remained a private enterprise. A number of trading posts, often referred to as forts, were established at many points along the river; they served as the source of the fur trade for years. When the army does construct its line of posts along the big muddy it contracts with private steamboat owners for transportation.

The W Bar Spread

Pierre Wibaux was born and raised in France, the son of a wealthy textile mill owner. However, his relationship with his father ended when he announced that he wanted to be an American cowboy, not a French factory owner. Daddy wrote a check for the equivalent of $10,000 and told him that was all he would receive.

For Pierre that was enough. His first stop in the United States was Chicago, working for a time in the stockyards to learn the cattle trade. In 1883 he partnered with Gus Grisy in a new ranching enterprise in Eastern Montana territory. Over the next three years the ranch prospered, Wibaux bought out his partner and built a large white painted home that some referred to as a Palace. The one story home sheltered in a grove of trees just outside the town that now bears his name.

When the winter of 1886 caused the big die off of cattle the W Bar ranch was hit as hard as any in the region. However Pierre looked at the disaster as an opportunity. He traveled to France to borrow money from relatives, he returned with $400,000 in cash and a promissory note to pay off $1 million dollars in 10 years. Wibaux used the money to buy out the surrounding ranchers and the stock that had survived the winter. While this allowed the W Bar to expand it also allowed some of the surrounding ranchers to salvage something from their ruined enterprises.

At its peak in the mid 1890's the W Bar ran an estimated 65,000 head of cattle and 300 saddle horses. The spring brandings tallied as many as 10,000 head of new calves making it the largest cattle ranch in America at the time. Its range straddled the Montana, North Dakota border with approximately two thirds of the land in the Dakotas.

The W Bar was sold off in the early 1900's; homesteaders were taking over the land, ending the free-range days and the cattle empire of Pierre Wibaux. Today just a bit west of the town of Wibaux, Montana stands a statue of Pierre Wibaux, a tribute to the man who made an empire out of the western grasslands of the Great Plains.

Where'd That Horse Wander Off To

Theodore Roosevelt seemed fascinated by the winter weather of the Badlands. He writes that the 'great white landscape' seemed like another land. He also offers that the snow covered countryside made identifying landmarks difficult, making it tricky to navigate.

There were many reasons for a rancher or cowboy to be out on the range during the winter. You might be one of the line-riding cowboys whose daily job was to ride the ranch border turning cattle back on to the proper range. You might be hunting or bringing supplies to the outlying operations of your ranch. Or you might, as TR found himself doing, be out looking for a lost horse.

Teddy spent several days riding along Beaver Creek looking for the wayward equine. During that time he met and befriended a Texas cowboy who was out on the same mission. While the weather was mild during the early part of this horse-hunting trip it deteriorates into a white out blizzard as the pair heads for their homes. Roosevelt was forced to rely on compass bearings to maintain their headings on the trail for nearly nine hours.

Fortunately for the unlikely pair they came across an abandoned cabin near Sentinel Butte. There they rode out the storm, passing the time with Teddy reading aloud from a pocket copy of Hamlet that he had packed in his saddlebag. The Texas cowboy commented at the end of the evening that 'old Shakespeare sure savvied human nature'.

The west was made up of people of all walks of life; some cowboys had little or no education and some were educated in the finest schools in the country. This mix made the west a greater melting pot than any other part of the country, and makes for our fascination with the lives and legends of the time.

An Underground Marriage

It was a wedding made for the punsters when on May 3, 1920 vows were exchanged in the Garden of Eden room of the Wind Cave. Some felt that they were running matrimony right into the ground, even the bride and groom joined in the witty remarks. They said that by marrying in a cave they were starting at the bottom and the marriage could go nowhere but up.

Despite all the puns and bad jokes the marriage lasted, in 1958 Mr. and Mrs. H. C. Magorian celebrated their 38th wedding anniversary with a trip back to Wind Cave.

Weddings did not become a common occurrence at Wind Cave. A search of the web site found mention of just the one 'underground ceremony'. Even that was enough to cause the renaming of the room as the 'Bridal Chamber'.

I am sure that many people would consider the uniqueness of a cave wedding for their nuptials. They might enjoy the beauty of the cave or just crave an event that is different from all the other weddings that they have attended.

But the most interesting reason for a wedding ceremony in the depths of the earth came from the original bride herself. She stated that she had promised her mother that she would marry no man on the face of the earth. By exchanging vows in a cave, deep below the face of the earth, she was keeping her word to her sainted mother and joined her new husband.

Doughboys, Doctors and Nurses

For North Dakotans the call to the serve for the First World War was heeded quickly no matter what their feelings towards the politics of the conflict. In all over 31,000 men served their country with more than half voluntarily enlisting. Even those North Dakotans who were drafted excelled, 78% of the state's draftees passed the physical compared to a 70% national average.

This exodus of young men lowered college enrollments by 11% in 1918. This at a time when the colleges were starting the new Student Army Training Corps, the forerunner of the Reserve Officer Training Corps, or ROTC of today.

But North Dakota did not just furnish volunteers for the military. People volunteered for the YMCA, which entertained the troops overseas, others worked in libraries at posts in Europe, and some, including former governor Louis Hanna, worked with the Red Cross in France.

The biggest volunteer effort came from Bismarck, Dr. Eric Quain, already the founder of a clinic, organized a Red Cross Hospital Unit made up of Doctors and nurses from the capital city. This unit became a base hospital in France taking care of the wounded doughboy. Dr. Quain became the chief of surgery and the director of Operating Teams for all American Hospitals in France.

In all nearly 150 North Dakota nurses and 200 physicians served the medical needs of the American soldier in the trenches of Europe. They were sorely needed.

Just over 1300 North Dakota soldiers lost their lives in World War One, about half from wounds and half from disease. Wounds and diseases that were treated by volunteers from North Dakota in those far away lands.

Wages and Retirement

For the most part, the early explorers and settlers of the region were an independent lot, generally working for themselves as they made their lives on the Dakota Plains. But there were a few major companies that employed many people on the prairies.

Obviously, in the early days these companies were all involved in the fur trade. One of the major players in this trade, especially away from the Missouri River, was the Hudson Bay Company.

Chartered in England the Hudson Bay Company was the Canadian equivalent of the East India Company. While the East India Company traded in tea and other luxuries from India the Hudson Bay Company dealt in furs.

And they treated their employees quite well. Even in the 1840's and 50's they paid their clerks the princely wage of the equivalent of $500 per year. Managers, or factors as they were known, made twice as much.

But the biggest benefit to employment with the Hudson Bay Company was its profit sharing plan. After ten years a clerk was given a share of the profits, factors were given two shares.

Even in the middle of the 19th century a share of profit was reported to be worth $10,000 per year. Not a bad retirement, after ten years of service a pension worth twenty times your annual salary.

It was the first, and probably the best, 401k in the Dakotas. Not only did this compensation plan draw some highly competent workers to the Hudson Bay Company payroll, it often provided for a class of 'gentlemen farmers' that spent their retirements on farms surrounding the fur trading posts of their former employer.

Take Ten Paces and Check Your Shirt

Henry Clay was born in Virginia in 1777, just one year after the Declaration of Independence. He was active in politics for much of his 75 years, rising from the Kentucky House of Representatives in 1803 to serve in the United States Senate in 1806. His political career also included a stint as the United States Secretary of State from 1825 to 1829 and runs for the Presidency in 1824 and 1832 as a National Republican and in 1844 as a Whig.

In all he served a total of 29 years as either a Senator or Congressman from the State of Kentucky, an impressive record of service for a man that will come to be known as 'The Great Compromiser' for his part in adopting the Missouri Compromise. Clay, a slave owner, was instrumental in drafting the legislation in 1821 that kept the United States from being torn apart by Civil War for more than 40 years.

But in at least one incident Henry Clay did not compromise. In 1809 Clay introduced a bill in the Kentucky House of Representatives mandating that legislatures could only wear clothing made from homespun cloth, not the fine cottons imported from England. I suppose it could be viewed as a matter of American pride in the time between the War for Independence and the War of 1812.

But at least one of Clay's fellow state legislatures didn't like the idea of dressing in the coarser American attire. Humphrey Marshall was so adamantly opposed to the prohibition against English fabric that he and Henry Clay ended up fighting a duel over the issue.

Neither is killed in the exchange of gunfire although both were wounded. The Code de Duella required the affair to end when either party is 'blooded'. Henry Clay lives until 1852, counties in 15 states, including South Dakota and Minnesota are named in his honor.

A Quick Game of Billiards

General Philip de Trobriand was a Frenchman who had served with distinction during the American Civil War. At the end of the rebellion he returned to France to write his memoirs of the war. But in 1868 he returned to the United States Army and was placed in command of Fort Buford, Fort Totten, and his headquarters, Fort Stevenson, which was still under construction.

One of the first things he did was tour the posts in his command including the Indian Agency Fort Berthold. It was there that he saw some Indian children playing a game that his fellow officers referred to as 'Billiards'.

There were two teams of two players. Each had a stick, about six feet long that all the bark had been removed from except for three bands, one at each end and one in the middle. The other piece of this game was a round, flat stone with a hole in the middle.

One team member from each squad would stand at each end of a flat area. A player would roll the rock towards the other end of the field. Once it crossed a certain point each participant would anticipate where the rock would stop and throw their stick as close to that point as possible.

The stick with its middle band of bark closest to the rock won a point. The players from the other end of the field would then repeat the action in the other direction.

General de Trobriand did not give us the Indian name of the game in his journal. My guess is that the Americans gave it the name of 'Billiards' for the resemblance of the sticks used in the game to cue sticks. The General stated that many of the players were so skillful that the round often ended with the rock wheel resting on one of the sticks when it stopped.

Chalk One Up for the Indians

The first cattle drives in the Dakotas were from army fort to army fort moving the cattle that would serve as food for the soldiers through the winter. In July of 1868 Lt. Cussick led a detail of fifty soldiers in herding over two hundred head of cattle from Fort Stevenson to Fort Buford along the Missouri River in what is now Northwestern North Dakota.

While Indians made a few attempts at cutting the herd they enjoyed little success. They decided to make a more concerted effort at acquiring some of what they referred to as 'pinto buffalo'.

On August 20th, while the cattle grazed within a mile and a half of the fort, the Indians struck. The 25 mounted infantrymen on herd duty were quickly overrun. While reinforcements rushed from Fort Buford it was too late. Of the 250 beefs that had been grazing only forty remained, most of those had been wounded in the exchange.

Lt. Cussick led a mounted charge to try to reclaim the cattle. He, along with eight mounted soldiers, charged the Sioux and Cheyenne warriors but were repelled by flights of arrows, one of which lodged in the Lieutenant's saddle. However, Cussick's only injury was a club blow to the back from a warrior counting coup.

Most of the action occurred so close to Fort Buford that the post surgeon watched from the walls. Like a good ringside referee he rendered a decision on the fight, stating that in his opinion the Indians had 'won the day'.

The official tally of the day was 192 cattle and four horses taken along with two soldiers killed and two wounded. While no records of Indian casualties exist, it would appear that on that August day the Indians did 'win the day', and the pinto buffalo.

Let's Have the Neighbors Over

The writings of McKay and Evans as well as the stories heard along the river by Captains Lewis and Clark had established the Mandan Villages as the center of commerce and trade along the Missouri. During the late summer and early fall the Mandan and Hidatsa Villages became the Kmart of the prairie. Indians from as far away as the Rocky Mountains journey to the Missouri River to trade amongst themselves as well as with English traders.

These villages were so well known that the Corps of Discovery had planned to winter near the Mandans for the winter of 1804 – 1805. By mid October the Corps was passing abandoned Mandan Villages along the shores, Small Pox had already had a tragic effect.

On October 24, 1804 the Lewis and Clark expedition meets its first Mandan. Sheheke, or Big White as he was more commonly known, and a hunting party of 25 men are encountered. Two days later the expedition camped just below the southern of the two Mandan villages. While the Mandan and Hidatsa are friendly the Captains take no chances. They determine that either Captain Lewis or Clark will remain at the boat at all times while the other visits in the village. Villages populated by nearly 4,000 people and with 1,300 of them warriors.

The last days of October are spent in councils with the Chiefs of the nearby Indian villages but also in meetings with an English trader named Hugh McCracken. When McCracken leaves on November 1st he carries with him an invitation to other English traders to visit Fort Mandan during the upcoming winter. In fact several French and English frontiersmen will visit the Corps over the next months making the 150-mile journey from the North West Company posts along the Assiniboine River.

Hook Mama to the Travois

It had been used to transport the camp equipment of the Northern Plains Native Americans for centuries. Two long poles fastened at the withers of a horse and trailing back on the ground behind the animal. At the end of this arrangement a platform was created by lashing together branches with rawhide.

Not only was gear transported on the travois but the poles used were also the Tipi poles that made up the home of these nomads. As you would expect constant dragging wore down the wood. After seasons of travel the tipi would actually become shorter from the wear.

While the common picture we have of the travois is horse drawn, this transportation tool of the Indian was in use eons before equines made their appearance on the Northern Plains.

So what pack animal provided the power to move an Indian Camp in the day before the horse? Dogs were commonly used, but they required shorter poles and could move fewer goods.

But there was one other draft animal available to the Native Americans. The women of the tribe were also expected to harness themselves to the travois and move the camp.

It must have been a great advance for Indian Society when they acquired horses. They could move their camps more quickly and efficiently. And mama didn't have to haul the tent all by herself.

Tote that Bag

On June 15, 1868 General de Trobriand accompanied the sternwheeler the 'War Eagle' to Fort Berthold to distribute the annuity goods to the Indians gathered there. Word that the steamer was on its way had already reached the natives. The Chiefs were gathered at the river bank in full dress including war bonnets. Some of the Hidatsa and Arikara warriors were even painted for battle to signify their recent victory over the Sioux.

But despite the pageantry of the Indian men gathered on the shore de Trobriand wanted to get on with the job of unloading the War Eagle of the supplies meant for the Indians and reloading it with some left over oats that was to be transported back to Fort Stevenson.

With just three wagons and ten men to make the transfer the General quickly calculated that it would take days to move all the goods. Knowing that the Indian men would consider loading and unloading wagons beneath their station in life, de Trobriand ordered his translator to recruit fifty or sixty women instead.

But it seems the translator carried the orders a little further than General de Trobriand intended. Instead of just loading and unloading the wagons the Indian women were soon carrying the bags of oats, some weighing as much as 130 pounds, on their backs the six hundred yards from the warehouses to the boat. The feedbags were secured to the women by two rawhide straps, one across the forehead and one across the upper chest.

While de Trobriand claimed in his journals that he never intended the women to carry the heavy bulky goods themselves he does not stop their work. For two and half days they labor under the hot Dakota sun moving over four thousand bags of feed.

And for this heavy labor the General paid the sixty women three barrels of biscuits, about 120 pounds of bacon and thirty bags of moldy oats saying that oats not fit for army mules was still fit for Indians.

A Horse, Of Course

Columbus sailed the Ocean Blue in 1492 and it wasn't long until horses also crossed the Atlantic. By 1540 the Spanish had quite a herd in South and Central America, and the first recorded incident of horse theft by Indians.

Over the next two centuries these animals were raided and traded from tribe to tribe starting in the American Southwest. The Apache preferred his equine roasted not ridden across the land. By 1750 even the most remote tribes, such as the Blackfoot of Northern Montana, had acquired riding stock. In fact, some estimates place the number of horses in North America at nearly 3 million head at the time of the Lewis and Clark expedition.

So when did the Plains tribes such as the Sioux, Mandan, and Hidatsa acquire horses? Probably right around 1700. This was also about the time that the Sioux arrived at the Missouri River. Originally the homeland of the Sioux had been along the headwaters of the Mississippi in what is now northern Minnesota. They were forced west by eastern tribes that had been displaced by the early colonists on the east coast.

The changes in the lifestyle of the Sioux must have been immense. They had to learn how to survive on the open prairie after centuries in the north woods. Add to this the acquisition of the greatest tool for transportation, warfare and hunting and you can understand the changes that occurred.

Within a couple of generations the Sioux had made the Great Plains their home. They were nomadic, relying on the horse to move their camps after the buffalo. They were the mounted warrior society that would fight the United States Army for nearly thirty years.

We're Out Here for the Hats

You might call it the rodent that opened the west. Long before the first pilgrim settlers arrived on the North American shores the felt top hat became the fashion for gentlemen of style in Europe. The highest quality felt for these hats was made from the under fur of the beaver.

By 1600 the beaver was all but extinct in Europe and over the next century the streams of Scandinavia and Russia will be trapped out as well. This left the North American continent as the only source for beaver fur.

The large rodent, they often weighed 25 to 40 pounds, was plentiful in the woods of the East Coast of the new continent in Colonial days but they also succumbed to hunting and trapping pressure.

This left the American west as the last source for the beaver. By the early 1800's the Lewis and Clark expedition had explored the west but it was the quest for 'plews' or beaver hides that brought the Mountain Man, the west's first white residents to the region.

While beavers may be nature's engineers and capable of construction of dams and lodges they were remarkably easy to trap. They could be lured into the steel jaws simply by placing a stick marked with a potion made from the beaver's sex glands above it.

The term 'Mountain Man' was applied to these fur trappers although some spent their time on the plains and many of the important trading posts of this era were along the Missouri River in the Dakotas.

Just as in Europe, Scandinavia, Russia and the Eastern United States the beaver was trapped to near extinction in the American west in the course of about 50 years. By 1845 the aquatic rodent was as scarce in this region as in Europe. But this time the trappers didn't move onto other streams. By the 1850's the silk hat had replaced the beaver felt hat as the head gear of choice for men of fashion.

But for many of the trappers and traders the lure of life in the American West outlasted the fickle fashions of Europe. These Mountain Men and traders stayed in the mountains and on the plains, becoming the guides to the emigrant wagon trains and the buffalo hunters that made up the next generation of the American westward expansion.

In the course of a generation the American West is explored and mapped not by the government but by individuals in quest of a rodent, the lowly beaver.

A Massacre in the Snow

The American Indians call it the 'Chief Big Foot Massacre'; the white historians refer to it as the 'Wounded Knee Massacre'. Either way you look at it the word 'Massacre' stands out.

The confrontation on December 29, 1890 was the culmination of a series of events. Earlier in the year the 'Ghost Dance Craze' had started with a single medicine man in Nevada. It travels from tribe to tribe fostering the belief that those who believe will become impervious to the white man's bullets. Many of the Sioux in the Dakotas become active believers in the Ghost Dance. A belief that made the residents of the newly admitted states of North and South Dakota nervous.

Ghost Dance participation led to the death of Sitting Bull during his arrest attempt in early December. Later that month Chief Big Foot and 350 Sioux were under the guard of the 7th Cavalry at Wounded Knee Creek. On December 29, 1890 Colonel James Forsyth ordered that these Indians be disarmed of all guns, knives, axes and even tent stakes. While these weapons are being piled a shot rings out.

This single shot is followed by volleys of shots from the carbines of the 7th cavalry and the rapid fire Hotchkiss Gun they had stationed on a nearby hill. This piece was capable of firing nearly a shot per second into the Indians gathered below.

When the massacre ended half of the Indians lay dead in the snow. Many wounded crawled into the brush and perished in the sub zero December weather. Overall an estimated 300 of the original 350 Sioux men, women and children lost their lives. The 7th Cavalry casualties were 25 killed in a battle that they considered retribution for the Battle of the Little Bighorn.

Hot Time in the Old Town

When any new town is founded one of the first tasks is to give it a name. When the residents of Armour, South Dakota chose that name they were honoring Philip Armour. Not only was he on the board of directors of the Milwaukee Railroad but, of course, the head of the Armour Meat Packing Company.

The community prospered with a thriving business center including a number of liveries, saloons, restaurants, and even a cigar maker and a racetrack. Unfortunately eighteen of those businesses burned in 1891 prompting the formation of a volunteer fire department in 1892.

They must have been a busy bunch of firefighters; the city was plagued by fires in 1916, 1926, 1931, 1932, 1934, 1952, and in 1959. Each of these major fires claiming a little more of the small community.

So did the community of Armour, South Dakota get an 'Armour Meat Packing Company' packing plant? They must have hoped that such a business might locate in a town named for the company's founder.

The town never did become home to a major slaughterhouse, but it did receive something from Philip Armour. Shortly after the town's founding in 1886 he donated a church bell for the steeple of the first house of worship in the community. A bell that they might have rung to alert the fire department.

A Little Cabin at the Worlds Fair

Just a couple months after Sitting Bull was killed by the Indian Police another conflict erupted over the possessions of the late Lakota leader. Lyman Casey, a hardware store owner from Carrington, was one of North Dakota's first United States Senators. In February of 1891, Casey began lobbying the Federal Indian Department to turn over Sitting Bull's possessions to the state of North Dakota.

It would be nice to think that the intent of this collection was for historic preservation. Unfortunately that was not the purpose behind North Dakota acquiring the very cabin that Sitting Bull had lived in.

With the aid of Standing Rock Indian Agent James McLaughlin, the state of North Dakota negotiated the purchase of the cabin from Sitting Bull's widows. The log building was then dismantled and removed from its Grand River, South Dakota location.

So what did North Dakota do with this historic structure? Well, they used it for marketing the state. The cabin was reconstructed as the centerpiece of the North Dakota exhibit at the Chicago World's Fair in 1892.

Thousands of people stopped at the North Dakota display to see the home of the man whose name was most connected with the defeat of General Custer and the 7th Cavalry along the Little Bighorn River in Montana.

But the state of North Dakota was not the only one to attempt to use Sitting Bull's fame. Just five years before his death the Hunkpapa chief had spent a season touring with Buffalo Bill's Wild West Show.

All reports are that Sitting Bull and Bill Cody got along well; they even had their photo taken together at Montreal, Canada in 1885. At the end of the season Buffalo Bill gave Sitting Bull the horse that the Lakota Chief had ridden during the show. He also paid to have the gray horse transported from St. Louis, where the show wrapped up the season, to Sitting Bull's Grand River home.

The horse continued to be the Lakota Chief's favorite mount. Sitting Bull even called for this pony when Indian Police officers came to arrest him. Unfortunately this arrest turned into a gunfight that took the life of Sitting Bull and nearly ten others all while the grey horse, remembering his old Wild West show days, stomped and counted and went through his show routine.

So what happened to this favorite horse of the Lakota Chief? Early in 1891 Buffalo Bill purchased the horse from the widows of Sitting Bull and returned him to the Wild West Show. Cody rode the grey during the Grand Entrance parade of his show for several years including the performances in Chicago in 1892 at the World's Fair. Who knows, it is possible that the grey once again did its tricks outside the cabin of Sitting Bull, but this time in Chicago, Illinois. Not along the Grand River of South Dakota.

Where Do You Want Me to Park the House?

From time to time the early settlers of the Dakotas would find it necessary to move lock, stock and barrel to another location. Often it was the result of better land becoming available. Often, if it wasn't very far, the pioneers moved their houses to the new home site.

Near Highmore, South Dakota Bart Mitchell, the local house mover, had acquired the latest in house moving equipment. First the building was jacked up, in the days before electrical power and plumbing it wasn't as difficult as it would be now, and timbers were attached to the home. Metal rollers would be placed under these timbers.

The power to move the house came from a horse powered winch. This winch was staked to the ground as a horse walked around it winding up a cable attached to the house. As the building moved forward workers would move the metal rollers from behind the house to in front of the structure.

In order for this one horsepower machine to move a house it had to be geared very low. In fact this rig wasn't going to set any land speed records. In a six day work week a house could be moved all of a half of a mile.

In at least one case the house moved so slowly that the family continued to live in it. The farm wife continued all the household chores of washing, cooking and even baking bread while her home was moving across the plains to its new location.

Army Discipline vs. Tribal Discipline

Captains Lewis and Clark had relatively few discipline problems during the Corps of Discovery. Problems they did have were generally dealt with quickly and severely. Earlier in the expedition Private Moses Reed had attempted to desert, his punishment had included a whipping as well as discharge from the army. Unfortunately with the Corps nearly a thousand miles from the nearest American outposts former Private Reed was forced to travel with the expedition.

Reed was still a malcontent, complaining about his harsh treatment by the officers to anyone who would listen. His outbursts had the most effect on Private John Newman, inciting the young soldier to his own outburst resulting in the arrests of both Newman and Reed.

While Reed was no longer subject to military discipline Newman was. On October 13, 1804 he was charged with 'uttering repeated expressions of a highly criminal and mutinous nature'. Even though Newman pleads not-guilty the court-martial found him guilty and sentenced him to seventy-five lashes to be administered at noon the next day and expulsion from the army.

Witnessing the punishment was not only the entire Corps of Discovery but also a Chief of the Arikara Indians. The chief was very alarmed by the punishment, actually crying out as the first lash is laid on. Captain Clark explained that it was sometimes necessary to establish discipline by example. The Chief told Captain Clark that when it was necessary to set an example he killed them rather than whipped them.

Both Reed and Newman were discharged from the Corps of Discovery and sent back to St. Louis the next spring, in the meantime they labored with the hired French boatman and were prohibited from carrying weapons.

Hauling a Heavy Load

After North and South Dakota were formed by an Act of Congress in 1889 an effort was made to mark the border. South Dakota Senator Richard Pettigrew introduced a bill in Congress appropriating $25,000 to survey and mark the division line between Uncle Sam's new twins. During the years of 1891 and 92 an impressive series of quartzite markers were to be placed every half mile along the border.

These red quartzite markers, quarried near Sioux Falls, South Dakota, were shaped into seven foot tall, ten inch square pillars weighing approximately 880 pounds. They were marked on three sides, with ND chiseled on the North side, obviously SD on the South side and either the distance from the Minnesota border on the markers placed at the whole mile or 1/2 mile on the markers placed in between. To aid in surveying, the Standard Corners of Townships were also marked with the township number.

Placing these markers was a mammoth task. A transit with a solar attachment was used to take sightings on the Sun and North Star. This allowed the surveyors to calculate the longitude to determine the mileage from the Minnesota border and the latitude of the border.

While these calculations had to be painstakingly made, no Global Positioning Systems in those days, it pales in comparison to the efforts required just to get these monuments to the border. The stone pillars were transported by rail to the nearest railhead to the border; from there they were loaded on wagons to be hauled to the border. Each wagon, drawn by two teams of horses, could transport just five of the monuments. Nearly 300 wagon loads of the quartzite markers were transported over the two years of this unique project.

The border of North and South Dakota is the only border marked in such a manner in the United States.

Champagne for Everyone

When the executives of the Northern Pacific Railroad Company decided to expand their transportation network to the high seas they did so in a big way. In 1903 they launched the Minnesota, the largest ship afloat. Already under construction was another vessel of the same design, one hundred years ago the Dakota was christened.

As you would expect everyone who was anyone in the Dakotas turned out at New London, Connecticut for the grand ceremony. And the guest of honor, the lady who would break the bottle of champagne across the bow was a 17 year old beauty from Ellendale, North Dakota.

Mary Belle Flemington was hailed as the 'Diana of the Prairies' by the press. The teenager stood a statuesque 6 foot 3 and had been voted the 'prettiest girl in North Dakota' by her fellow students at UND.

The New York press had high praise for the tall girl who was just a few days short of her eighteenth birthday as well. Both she and the ship were pictured prominently in the New York papers. And while Mary Belle saw all the sights of the Big Apple she just looked down on 'little old New York'. After six days on the east coast she headed home, stating 'I wouldn't give my little garden in Ellendale, Dickey County, North Dakota with its broad vista of the prairie for all the palaces on Fifth Avenue'.

The responsibilities of christening a ship could be a bit daunting. The president of the construction company told Mary Belle that President Cleveland's wife shook so bad in fear that she couldn't perform her christening duties. After the braces were removed the ship could start sliding immediately or take a few moments to start its descent to the sea. Mary Belle was not to swing the bottle of champagne before the ship started moving but before the Dakota got out of reach.

At risk was the luck of the ship. The more pieces the bottle broke in to, the better luck the Dakota would have. If she missed the ship entirely sailors would hesitate to man her, fearing bad luck.

And They're Off

It probably started as a hoax, Dawes County Nebraska Clerk and sometimes newspaper correspondent John Maher had a flair for sending preposterous press releases to the eastern newspapers of the era. He had no plan for any sort of financial gain but just wanted to see if the New York Post would run his stories about things like a Petrified Man or the Alkali Lake Monster. In this vein Maher sent out a press release announcing a horse race from Chadron, Nebraska to the Columbian Exhibition in Chicago, Illinois.

By March the phantom race had generated so much publicity that Chadron community leaders organized a rules committee, set the entry fee at $25, the purse as $1000, and scheduled June 13, 1893 for its start. Additional prize money was added by Buffalo Bill's Wild West Show which would serve as the finish line in the windy city. Montgomery Ward added a Saddle and a Colt revolver to the winner's purse.

Each entrant could use only two stock horses, no thoroughbreds allowed, and had to ride a western saddle weighing at least 35 pounds. From the start Humane Societies across the country protested the contest. This probably caused the initial field of 24 entrants including one woman to dwindle to just nine at the start of the race.

As the riders traveled the course they drew a great deal of attention. People followed on horseback and even bicycles to get a glimpse of the horsemen on the 1000 mile race. As they approached the checkpoint at Sioux City, Iowa, spectators took their seats along a levee a full 24 hours before the horses arrived to ensure a good seat.

In 13 days and 16 hours John Berry of Sturgis, South Dakota crossed the finish line winning the Buffalo Bill prize money and a Montgomery Ward Saddle. He was not awarded any of the Chadron Prize money amid allegations of shipping his horses part way by rail. The Nebraska referee gave the top prize to a Nebraska rider, Joe Gillespie of Coxville, Nebraska.

But the real winner of the race might be the horse ranchers of the American West. Ed Lemmon in his autobiography 'Boss Cowman' felt that the horses and horsemen of the race performed so well that they attracted attention as far away as Europe. This led to England, France, and other countries sending buyers to the Great Plains to purchase remounts for their Cavalry units.

Ride'em Hollywood Cowboy

Harding County of western South Dakota and its county seat of Buffalo have never been what one would call crowded. Even at the peak of its population in 1925 it boasted just over 3500 people scattered over nearly 2600 square miles. Today Harding County's population density is well below one person per section.

But that is not to say that this region has not produced a notable athlete. Back around World War I and in the years that followed a horse by the name of 'Tipperary' was considered one of the greatest bucking horses in the world.

From 1915 to 1928 he was the featured bucking horse at the Tri-State Roundup in Belle Fourche as well as at other major rodeos around the area. In fact just three cowboys made the claim of having ridden Tipperary and even those rides were debated by rodeo fans for years. One of those making the ten second whistle that rodeo used back in those days was a local Belle Fourche cowboy by the name of Harold Ekberg.

But another rider that made a qualified trip came from Hollywood. Yakima Cannut was a rodeo champion from Washington who had been invited to work as a stuntman by none other than Tom Mix. Over the years he will double for the likes of John Wayne, Clark Gable and almost every other leading man of Hollywood. He even acted in some movies before they found his voice was not right for the new 'talkie' movies. By his own admission he sounded like a 'hillbilly in a well'. In later years Cannut was considered the best director of action scenes in movies. Many consider his direction of the twenty minute long chariot race scene in 'Ben Hur' his greatest effort.

Yakima Cannut was awarded an Oscar in 1966 for his work as a stuntman and stunt coordinator in countless films over the decades. Probably as big an accomplishment as his riding Harding County's Tipperary at Belle Fourche in 1920 and 1921.

Tipperary grazed out his later years near Buffalo, South Dakota. He died on the open range during a 1932 blizzard at the age of 22. He was buried under a plaque naming him the 'Greatest Bucking Horse Ever'. Yakima Cannut retired from movie making in 1976 and died in 1986. In his life he was honored not only with an Oscar, the first ever awarded to a stuntman, but by induction into the National Cowboy Hall of Fame.

A Native Frontier Army

Joseph R. Brown had a long history along the frontier of Minnesota and the eastern part of the Dakotas. The Brown's Valley area was named in his honor and his son, Samuel Brown, served as Chief of Scouts at Fort Sisseton and is best known for his ride in April of 1866 that gave him the reputation as the 'Paul Revere of the West'.

Old Joseph Brown was a frontiersman in his own right. He was part of General Sibley's expedition across the Dakota Territory in 1863 and may have been a participant in battles such as Big Mound and Buffalo Lake.

But in 1866 he had a different plan for fighting the Dakota War. He wrote a letter to General Sibley proposing that the forces of friendly Indians be used as soldiers against the hostiles. The only white troops that would accompany these forces were to be a few 'artillerists'.

Brown was so enthused about this plan that his letter stated that he would 'hang his hat, boots, and pantaloons' on it. He also pointed out that it was not an original idea. He was copying the tactics of the English in their battles in places like India and Algiers.

The military leaders of the day did not take Brown's advice to heart. Friendly Native Americans were consistently used as scouts but never as the main force against hostile forces.

Maybe our American society was not quite enlightened enough to trust its safety to an army of Native Americans. Certainly the population along the frontier, a population that very seldom differentiated between tribes, would have fought any such plan.

Dead Bill in Deadwood

While many mining towns sprang up in those early days of Black Hills settlement the queen of the boom towns was Deadwood. It boasted not only the richest mines in the area but the most active, and violent social life.

Bloodshed may have not been a daily occurrence but did happen with alarming regularity. One historian tallied 97 murders in the first three years of Deadwood's existence. Of course only one of these homicides has made it to the status of western legend. On August 2, 1876 James Butler 'Wild Bill' Hickok was shot down by Jack McCall.

How James Butler Hickok became 'Wild Bill' Hickok is a matter of historic speculation. It may have been a nickname earned during his days driving a stagecoach or possibly during his Civil War exploits. His reputation grew during his time as a lawman in Kansas. City officials in Abilene may have fired him for being just a bit too rough as he dispensed justice.

In any event, his own self-promotion while touring with Buffalo Bill's Western Tent Show seemed to expand his reputation and ultimately his legend. He never seemed to be restrained by the truth when relating his own exploits.

So how wild was 'Wild Bill' in Deadwood? Since he left Abilene he had lived the life of a professional gambler, and become a married man. Hickok had married Agnes Lake in Cheyenne, Wyoming on May 4, 1876. A month later the groom left for the Dakota Territory and just two days short of their three month anniversary he lay dead on the floor of the Number 10 saloon.

The Yellowstone Expedition of 1873

When the 7th Cavalry first moved to the Dakotas they weren't allowed to even get to their new post before they were sent into the field to protect the Northern Pacific Railroad surveyors as they explored the Dakota Badlands and the Yellowstone Valley.

Colonel Custer led the troops of the 7th west from Fort Rice, forty miles south of the still incomplete Fort Lincoln, in June of 1873. While the column was challenged by summer hail storms and the Dakota Badlands themselves at least the early part of the expedition seemed more like an extended hunting party than a military campaign.

Custer personally led 25 handpicked riflemen each day on hunting scouts providing not only meat for the troops but also specimens for him to mount and furnish to the natural history museums of the country.

While many of the officers of the 7th Cavalry and the 22nd Infantry spent their evenings drinking heavily, a common vice of the Frontier Army, Custer spent much of his time reminiscing and talking to new friends. The chief engineer for the Northern Pacific survey party was Tom Rosser, a good friend of Custer's from their time at West Point. They rekindled their friendship on the Dakota and Montana prairies after fighting on opposite sides during the recent Civil War. Rosser and Custer spent many evenings lying on a buffalo robe, staring into the starlit sky, exchanging war stories.

General Custer's friendship with one of the new officers of the expedition could be considered a bit unusual.

Fred Grant had graduated from West Point just two years earlier near the bottom of his class. Any other officer would have been a Second Lieutenant, but any other officer didn't have the First Lady as his mother.

Mrs. Grant had effectively lobbied General Sheridan, the commander of the Missouri District, that the President's son shouldn't hold such a low rank. He ultimately relented, placing Fred Grant on his staff with the rank of Lieutenant Colonel.

When Grant is assigned to Custer's 7th for the Yellowstone Expedition of 1873 you might expect that the young officer could be considered a debutante and have trouble with General Custer and the other officers of the expedition. But actually Custer found Grant a likeable, modest, and frank youth.

In fact Custer thought so much of Fred Grant that he instructed

Libbie, who was spending the summer in Monroe, Michigan, to meet his train as he traveled east after the expedition and invite him to have dinner at her home.

But maybe the boy General had a little political motivation for the dinner invite. He also instructed Libbie to make sure that she had President Grant's portrait hanging in the parlor when she entertained the young Colonel Fred Grant.

Grant was again assigned to the 7th for the Black Hills Expedition of 1874 but would not be associated with General Custer during the 1876 campaign against the Lakota. General Custer had been called to Washington early in the year to testify at Congressional hearings regarding Government corruption. One of the primary subjects of this testimony was Orville Grant, the President's brother. U. S. Grant had to be persuaded to allow Custer to lead the 7th, he wasn't about to send his son along for the ride.

Fred Grant continued his service to the United States Army. His first combat came during the Spanish American War in the Philippines in 1898. Upon his retirement from the military he followed his dad's footsteps into political service. He served as the United States Minister to Austria during the administration of Benjamin Harrison and as a New York City Police Commissioner.

Fred Grant died in 1912 at the age of 61.

Sending Out for Buffalo

The first Native Americans to be placed on the Crow Creek Reservation arrived in 1859 and were transferred from Yankton. Accompanying them was Reverend John Williamson who lived among the Indians while ministering and teaching them to read and write.

Unfortunately, the government did not supply enough rations. In fact, mass starvation seemed imminent if something wasn't done. Reverend Williamson hit upon the simplest solution. He requested that a hunting party be allowed to go out in pursuit of buffalo.

Indian Agent Colonel Clark Thompson took some convincing but he ultimately allowed the expedition only with the personal guarantee of Reverend Williamson that it would be peaceful and return to the reservation. The Minister not only made the guarantee but accompanied the hunting party on its trip west.

Historians disagree as to the number of hunters on this little trip; estimates vary from 100 to 800 warriors. They do agree that it was a rather poorly armed group with just ten rifles between them, the rest hunting with the traditional bow and arrow.

For three months the hunting party followed a herd of buffalo across the western South Dakota Plains. The nearly two thousand animals killed provided the meat and hides needed to see their people through what were starving times on the reservation.

At the end of the hunt, true to Reverend Williamson's word all the members of the hunting party returned to the reservation.

While the Indians not only provided for their own needs they did so at a lower cost than any government program. However, it was a lesson lost on the Indian Agents and their supervisors in Washington. There seems to be no other incident of Indians being allowed to provide for themselves.

A Prairie Temper Tantrum

It was the last great adventure that he ever undertook. In 1843 John James Audubon traveled the Missouri River to Fort Union on a research trip for what would become his final work, Quadrupeds of North America.

With the emphasis of this trip being mammals not birds you can guess some of the subjects that they pursued. Buffalo, elk, deer, badgers and even mice were drawn, painted, studied and hunted by the naturalist and his company.

But it was in pursuit of the antelope that Audubon and his fellow travelers may have looked the most ridiculous. Stories told by the hunters at the forts along the river related that antelope could be lured into range by waving a rag attached to the rifle ramrod. Indians even claimed that you could draw them close enough for an arrow shot by tying rags on your moccasins and lying on your back, kicking your feet in the air.

While the Native Americans employed a number of hunting methods, including ambushing the herds as they waded through rivers, luring seemed to be a favorite.

On July 21, 1843 somewhere along the Missouri River in what is now western North Dakota John James Audubon and his traveling partner Edward Harris decided to give the Indian method of antelope hunting a try.

They tied rags to their feet, lay on their backs on the prairie and kicked. Over the next 20 minutes of kicking they brought the antelope buck to within 60 yards before they fired and missed their game. One of this country's great artists, acting like a dying bug on the prairie, and he even wrote about it in his book.

Old Enemies on the Prairie

The spite between George Armstrong Custer and William B. Hazen had its roots at the end of their time at West Point. Shortly after Custer's graduation but before his assignment to a unit he came across a fight between two cadets. Instead of breaking up the fisticuffs, he cleared the area and refereed the bout. Not exactly military protocol. Custer was arrested by the officer of the day William B. Hazen.

Their paths crossed again in 1868 in Kansas when Generals Sheridan and Custer were in hot pursuit of some Kiowa Indians. Near Fort Cobb, Brevet General Hazen sent word that the Indians were peaceful, forcing Custer and Sheridan to reluctantly break off pursuit.

While these and other conflicts made for open animosity between the two Civil War Veterans the worst clashes came in 1874. Hazen was commander of Fort Buford, near present day Williston, and Custer commanded Fort Lincoln, near present day Bismarck. The two generals fought a war of words in the newspapers of the day.

Custer wrote glowing reports of the Dakotas largely at the behest of the Northern Pacific Railroad. They provided him with gifts such as tents, gave him free passage on their passenger trains and even put together a special train to move the General and Libbie through a Dakota Blizzard.

Hazen had no vested interest in promoting the Dakotas, and most likely just liked to disagree with the boy General. He wrote an article that ultimately ended up in the New York Times with the headline 'Worthless Railroad Land' where he described the Dakota land as not worth 'a penny an acre'.

The war of words continued between the two Dakota Generals in the nation's newspapers in what became a nationwide controversy over the value of the land in the northern Dakotas.

Custer penned a rebuttal to the Hazen article that appeared in the Minneapolis Tribune in April of 1874. His portrayal of the Dakotas continued the Northern Pacific's characterization of the region as the 'Northern Tropical Belt'.

In 1875 Hazen upped the ante by writing a book entitled 'Our Barren Lands'. He also made the feud a little more personal. Hazen wrote and published at his own expense a pamphlet entitled 'Some Corrections of My Life on the Plains', Custer's book about the 7th Cavalry's battle with the Cheyenne along the Washita.

While the crux of this war of words was the Railroad lands along the Northern Pacific Railroad the NPRR was in no position to take any actions. Bank failures had bankrupted the Northern Pacific in 1873, during the years of this exchange of verbage between the Dakota Generals; the railroad was financially unable to extend its track beyond it western terminus at Bismarck.

Custer's Gold

First we're going to tell you that this story is probably more legend than fact. My guess is that most tales of lost riches are, especially when they're more than 125 years old.

You have to believe that in 1876, during the middle of the hostilities with the Sioux in Montana, the army would send a supplemental payroll of gold coins from Bozeman, Montana to Fort Lincoln at Bismarck, North Dakota.

Gil Longworth, the wagon driver, and his two army guards were traveling near the Little Bighorn River and growing more fearful of the Indians that were all around them. Their level of fear continued to grow until they happened upon Captain Marsh and the Far West tied up along the river.

Longworth hit upon a solution. They left the gold on the Far West and tried to return to Bozeman. Legend continues that Longworth and his guards were all killed by Indians, which lead the military to believe that the gold had been taken by the natives.

But the legend continues that Captain Marsh and his two most trusted officers didn't want the gold on board as they traveled the rivers moving supplies and ultimately returned to Fort Lincoln with the wounded of Major Reno's command.

They supposedly cached the payroll gold in a cave on pine covered ridge above the Little Bighorn River about 15 miles above its mouth. Quotations from the Far West's Journal indicate that on the night of June 26, 1876 a wheelbarrow was used to transfer the gold and that the operation took about three and a half hours. The legend maintains that this gold has never been recovered.

As in all good 'lost riches story' there are many unexplained details. Little things like why didn't Captain Marsh or any of his officers return for the gold?

So if your travels take you to Montana, maybe to see the Little Bighorn Battlefield, and you happen upon a cave full of gold, remember where you heard this tale of riches and send me a tip.

Wild Times in Dickinson

In 1902 Ed Lemmon, the manager of the Sheidley Ranch leased a little pasture land from the Sioux on the Standing Rock Reservation. 865,429 acres of prime grazing was enclosed by a three strand barbed wire fence totaling 270 miles. At the time it was the largest pasture anywhere in the world.

As you would expect a large pasture takes a large amount of cattle to stock it. According to Lemmon's biography 'Boss Cowman' in 1905 he had arranged for the delivery of 1700 Oregon two year old steers to Dickinson by rail to be herded South to the pasture.

While Dickinson had been a major livestock shipping station for many years it had been some years since a trail crew complete with chuck wagon had arrived in town. The community welcomed them and hoped they wouldn't run over any women or children or shoot out any plate glass windows while there.

The crew of eleven cowboys arrived only to find that the shipment of cattle had been delayed. Cowboys of the day looking to pass the time generally looked in a saloon. They also ran into an old acquaintance by the name of Connie Huffman, a lady who had worked in the personal entertainment industry of the Dakotas for several years. In fact she had been so highly thought of during her days in Deadwood that the area cowboys had given her a silk dress with all the brands of the regions ranches embroidered on it.

Well, to make a long story short the cattle didn't arrive in Dickinson from Oregon for two weeks. That would be fourteen days of eleven cowboys on what must have been one wild time. When the cowboys finally headed for the stockyards to take the herd south the cook, Ed Comstock, was wearing the green silk embroidered dress as he drove the chuck wagon at a full gallop down Main Street of Dickinson.

Ranch manager Ed Lemmon took the whole incident in stride, until he started getting the bills. The Cowboys had charged over $450 to the ranch in meals, booze and rooms during their Dickinson bender. Ed tried to be fair about it, he divided the bill up amongst the crew and withheld it from their pay over the next months.

There's Gold in Them Thar Cats

Deadwood was a prosperous place in 1876. But along with the hordes of miners, gamblers and dancehall girls the new town had another, less savory, crowd to deal with. Even in its infancy it seems that Deadwood had a mouse problem

Thousands of people had rushed to the Black Hills area in the search for gold, most had packed just the bare necessities of life in order to get rich as quickly as possible. It seems that none had brought along a good old fashioned mouse hunting cat.

This created an opportunity for someone to make some money without having to dig for color. Legend has it that one 'Phatty' Thompson decided to capitalize on this feline shortage.

Phatty traveled to Cheyenne where he offered the street kids of the town a whole quarter for each stray cat they captured and brought him. Pretty fair wages for children when you consider that catching four pussy cats would earn you the equivalent of an adult's day's wages.

Once Phatty Thompson had a wagonload of kitties he headed for Deadwood, but not without incident. The wagon overturned near Hill City forcing wagon teamsters to roundup the scattered cats.

Despite the difficulties transporting felines was a profitable business. Legend says that Phatty sold the kitties for between $20 and $30 each and the Deadwood mouse population was never the same.

Look at Them Legs

Wind is one of the common plagues of the Great Plains. Imagine, if you will, that you are a modest young lady wearing the long hoop skirt of the day. Well, a gust of wind could expose much more of you than the morals of the day deemed appropriate.

In fact this very situation occurred on the parade ground of Fort Riley in Kansas when the 7th Cavalry was stationed there. The Boy General was not particularly happy when a gust of wind hiked Libbie's skirt, which measured a full 5 yards around, to at least half mast.

Legend has it that George Armstrong Custer himself hit upon the solution. He went to the post armory and acquired a number of lead bars that were meant to be melted into bullets for the Cavalry carbines. Instead he cut them into pieces and had them sewn into the hem of his wife's dress.

While this legend gives Custer credit for saving women's modesty all across the plains I'm sure that many others hit upon similar solutions. Other stories include using trace chains from worn out harness and even rocks as ballast to keep the fairer sex's ankles safe from the prying eyes of strange men.

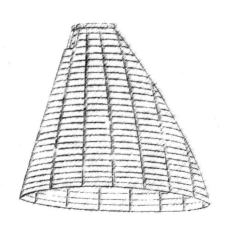

Set Em' Up Doc

Through the first 28 years of his life Doc Middleton, or James Riley as he had been born, had lived the life of a western outlaw. His prowess as a leader of a gang of horse thieves made him such a legend that the region of Nebraska frequented by his gang was known as 'Doc Middleton Country'. Over time he was captured and convicted of having the wrong equines in his possession.

He gained early release for good behavior from the Nebraska State Penitentiary in 1883 after serving less than four years of a five year sentence. This time he found occupations that didn't include herding other people's horses at night.

He married for the third time; no records exist of any divorces of his previous wives. He took part in the Chadron, Nebraska to Chicago, Illinois horse race in 1893 as a crowd favorite. He was a top three contender through the first half of the race but faded from contention after one of his horses was injured and finished towards the back of the pack.

He contemplated starting his own Wild West show; he had traveled with Buffalo Bill's show for several weeks after the Chadron race. And he even talked of going on the international lecture circuit with fellow reformed outlaw Frank James.

But most of Doc Middleton's later career was spent as a saloon keeper in Ardmore, South Dakota. For ten years, starting in 1903, Doc dispensed beer, whiskey and soda pop along with tales of the past glory of life as an outlaw in the old west.

It was not a life without tragedy, Middleton's wife died in 1911 and Doc seemed to get a yearning for the old days. In 1913 he moved to the new railroad boom town of Orin near Douglas, Wyoming. There he operated an illegal saloon or 'blind pig' as it was known.

After a knifing in the saloon outhouse attracted law enforcement attention Doc Middleton was arrested for selling alcohol without a license. He was found guilty and fined about $200 including court costs. In all likelihood he didn't have the money and instead ended up in jail. There he contracted a skin infection that claimed his life.

Doc Middleton, a legendary outlaw, horseman, and saloon keeper is buried in an unmarked grave in Douglas Park Cemetery at Douglas, Wyoming.

Maid Today, Bride Tomorrow

Fort Lincoln, near present day Mandan, North Dakota, was headquarters to the 7th Cavalry. With the flamboyant General Custer in command the post had become a bit of a showplace, a little luxury for the officers of the frontier army.

The post was well situated with access to supplies by both Missouri riverboat and Northern Pacific Railroad. This allowed the army and its officers to furnish the Fort with some of the nicer things available at the time.

For the wives of the married officers this meant a maid. With very few women in the area they turned to the east for these servants. A group of officers contracted with a Chicago employment agency to send some young women west to Fort Lincoln to work as maids along officer's row.

When these ladies arrived it caused quite a stir among the soldiers of the post. The troopers, starved for female companionship, started wooing the maids. Within two weeks the first was married and by the end of six weeks all had been wed.

The officers again contacted the Chicago employment agency. This time they requested that they be sent another bunch of maids, the homeliest girls possible, were specified.

That Chicago agency did its job well. It sent a bunch of women west that have been described as 'knock-kneed, cross eyed, and buck toothed'. They must have been about as homely as a mud fence. It took a full eight weeks for the last of them to become a bride.

The Little Phone Exchange on the Prairie

Alexander Graham Bell ushered in the age of telecommunications with those famous words 'Mr. Watson, Come here I want you' in 1876. That year Bell's fledgling company showed off the new invention at the Philadelphia Centennial Exposition where a Dakota Territory farmer saw them and acquired a pair.

J. L. Grandin, a successful Red River Valley bonanza farmer, operated several farms around the community that was named after his family. By 1877 he connected two of his farms by the new telephone. Over the next years he wired the rest of his farms even though the lines did not connect to the outside world.

The telephone remained a largely urban device while the Bell Telephone Company held the patent. When the patents expired in 1894 many companies began producing phones and related equipment. You could even buy instructions and equipment to construct a telephone exchange from the Montgomery Ward Catalog.

With sources for equipment readily available many people set out to meet the demands for telecommunications in the Dakotas. Over the years more than 800 companies operated exchanges in North Dakota. Many were family operations with the wife serving as the operator and the husband installing and maintaining the lines.

The early telephone was most often the 'magneto type'. The transmitter and receiver were held in a wooden cabinet along with the batteries and generator. You turned a crank attached to that generator to cause phones to ring all along the party line. The combination of long and short rings made up a code that specified who you were trying to call.

Some of those exchanges would have a special ring for all the members of the party line to pick up. They could then hear the weather forecast, market reports, and any other news that needed to be spread through the community. These local operators served the same role as the radio announcer in the days before radio.

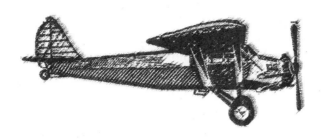

Flying North

Born and raised in Hatton, North Dakota Carl Ben Eielson was destined for the aviation history books. His flight training came from the Army Air Corps in 1918; Eielson then returned to North Dakota and graduated from the University of North Dakota in 1921 before turning to the skies of Alaska for adventure.

Sir Hubert Wilkins partnered with the young pilot for an historic exploration. The plan was to fly from Point Barrow, Alaska to Spitzbergen, Norway over the North Pole. Their first attempt in April of 1927 never headed north. During testing and exploration off the Alaskan north coast Eielson's plane was forced down by engine problems twice. Both times they managed to make repairs and take off but the ordeal had taken too heavy a toll on the fuel supply. Forced to land and abandon the plane Eielson and Wilkins walked for thirteen days covering over 125 miles on the polar ice to return to civilization. Frostbite forced the amputation of one of Carl's fingers and destroyed any chance for a cross polar flight that year.

But the next year went much better. On April 15, 1928 Carl Ben Eielson and Sir Hubert Wilkins took off from Point Barrow, Alaska. Their Lockheed Vega was loaded with 3000 pounds of fuel and twenty pounds of food, mostly chocolate. A little over twenty hours later rough weather forced them to land on an Island off the Norwegian coast. For five days they waited out the weather in their tiny aircraft before trying to take off.

The ice was so rough that Wilkins got out to push the plane. The plan, of course, was for him to jump back in before they got moving too fast. Imagine Eielson's amazement on taking off and looking back in the plane and not finding his partner. He landed, picked up Wilkins and tried the same plan again, and again left Sir Hubert on the frozen island.

On the third try they both got airborne. Wilkins had sat in the doorway of the plane and pushed with a piece of driftwood.

The intrepid pair of arctic explorers made news all around the world. The Englishman Hubert Wilkins was knighted by King George V and Eielson was awarded the Harmon Trophy, the highest American Aviation honor, by President Herbert Hoover.

A little over a year later they flew the same plane over the South Pole but for Carl Ben Eielson the fame was short lived. He died on November 9, 1929 in Siberia during a rescue effort of an ice bound ship. International search and rescue efforts were launched involving Russian, American, and Canadian forces. After 77 days the plane was located and nearly three weeks later the bodies of Eielson and his mechanic were found.

In March of 1930 Carl Ben Eielson's body was returned to Hatton, North Dakota for burial in what some still consider the state's biggest, and most memorable, funeral service.

Rumors of Our Death Are Greatly Exaggerated

I don't suppose there is anyway to figure out how the false news story got started but it certainly ended up in all the papers. Of course, it sounded like a sensational story.

The leading military publication of the day, *The Army and Navy Journal*, devoted most of its front page on April 6, 1867 to the story of a massacre. Many other newspapers, including the few in this region, carried the tale as well.

You see it was reported that the entire garrison of soldiers and their families at Fort Buford were massacred by Indians. The article even contained the gruesome detail that the wife of the post commander, Captain Rankin, had been killed by her husband to keep her from falling into the hands of the hostiles.

But the news stories gave the soldiers credit for making a valiant stand. The papers reported that over 300 hostile Indians had been killed before Fort Buford fell and every man, woman and child within was killed.

Fortunately, especially for Mrs. Rankin, the story was completely false. Winter weather had stopped all communications from the fort. With the coming of spring weather the rest of the world finally heard from Fort Buford. While there had been Indians around the post from time to time through the winter there had been no attacks.

It is possible the speculation of the post's demise was fueled by the last requests made by Captain Rankin to his superiors the previous fall. He had requested additional troops in order to stand the assault of the great number of Indians he knew were forthcoming. Obviously some reporter substituted his own imagination, and the Captain's fears, for reality.

By the middle of May newspapers all around the country were printing corrections. And Captain and Mrs. Rankin were dispelling rumors of their death.

The Ancient and Honorable Profession of Horse Stealing

James Riley was born in Texas in 1851 and got an early start up the outlaw trail. At the age of twenty he was indicted on charges of horse stealing, this was the first criminal charges leveled against Riley although there were rumors of at least three prior murders committed by him. Over the next five years a number of horse stealing charges were filed and eventually James Riley ended up in Huntsville Prison.

Once he was released from prison he worked as a drover on cattle drives from Texas to the Kansas trailheads before settling in Nebraska with a new name but an old profession.

By 1878 'Doc Middleton's Gang' was notorious for appropriating other people's horses in northwestern Nebraska and southwestern South Dakota. Some reports credit them with stealing nearly 2000 head. Many of these were taken from the reservations along the Missouri in the Dakota Territory. So many in fact that troops were added to keep the frontier safe from Indian raiders trying to steal their own ponies back.

With this type of wholesale crime the Government had to do something. In 1879 William Llewellyn and L. P. Hazen were recruited to capture Middleton and his gang. Hazen knew Doc, possibly from time in prison together, and was to introduce Llewellyn as a representative of the governor offering a pardon if Middleton stopped his horse stealing ways.

Even though Middleton was skeptical about the pardon, he retained a lawyer to contact the governor's office about it. If the offer was legitimate he could have his freedom in return for assisting detectives in apprehending other criminals.

Unfortunately, at least for Middleton, the pardon was bait in a trap. In an ambush Middleton is wounded along with both of his would be apprehenders. Doc Middleton escaped and lived to steal another day.

Accounts of the shootout varied. The outlaws portrayed the lawmen as back shooters and cowards under fire. The official reports of Llewellyn and Hazen portrayed their actions as a heroic attempt to serve justice against overwhelming odds.

We'll never know how that gunfight played out. We do know that Doc Middleton was captured a week later as he recovered from his wounds and in an early plea bargain agreement pled guilty to stealing three horses and was sentenced to five years in the Nebraska State Penitentiary.

An Officer and a Gentleman

Edward Godfrey may have ended his career as a Brigadier General but he started his days in the army as a private enlisting in an Ohio Volunteer Unit during the early days of the Civil War. Even while the War of the Rebellion continued Godfrey was singled out for admission to West Point graduating in 1867.

As a young Lieutenant in the 7th Cavalry he is detailed with Reno on their ill fated attack on the village. He survives the battle and is most often quoted for his descriptions of the Custer Battlefield after the Indians have fled.

But this would be only a small part of the career of Edward Godfrey. He is awarded the Medal of Honor for his actions at Bear Paw Mountain, Montana for leading his troops against Chief Joseph despite his own serious wounds in 1877.

He served in Cuba during the Spanish American War and in the Philippines during the Insurrection. He developed the drills and maneuvers used by the army cavalry in the later days of that service and wrote books about some of the classic campaigns of the Indian Wars including the Battle of the Little Bighorn. He was promoted to the rank of Brigadier General in early 1907 and retired later that year.

In 1921, at the age of 78 he led two companies of his fellow Medal of Honor winners as honor guards for the dedication of the Tomb of the Unknown Soldier at Arlington Cemetery. A body of a soldier 'known only to God' from World War I was interred there at that time.

Brigadier General Edward Godfrey died in 1932 and was laid to rest at Arlington Cemetery near the soldier he had helped honor eleven years earlier. Despite his long and illustrious career in the military the headline of his obituary still made note of him being a survivor of the 'Custer Massacre'.

Great Stories of the Great Plains - *Tales of the Dakotas - Vol. 1*
The radio show "Great Stories of the Great Plains" is heard on great radio stations all across both Dakotas. Norman has taken some of the stories from broadcasts, added some details, and even added some complete new tales to bring together this book of North and South Dakota history. Written by Keith Norman. (134 pgs.) $14.95 each in a 6x9" paperback.

Great People of the Great Plains Vol. 1
25 Biographies of People Who Shaped the Dakotas
This is the second book for Keith Norman and the first in this series. Keith has always had an interest in the history of the region. His radio show 'Great Stories of the Great Plains' is heard on great radio stations all across both Dakotas. While the biographies within this book are a bit too long to fit the time constraints of a radio show, listeners will find the events and people portrayed familiar. For more information on the radio show and a list of his current affiliates check out Norman's website at www.tumbleweednetwork.com. Written by Keith Norman - Author of *Great Stories of the Great Plains - Tales of the Dakotas* (124 pgs.) $14.95 each in a 6x9" paperback.

PLEASE SEND ME ADDITIONAL COPIES OF:

_____ **GREAT _STORIES_ OF THE GREAT PLAINS - VOLUME 1**

_____ **GREAT _STORIES_ OF THE GREAT PLAINS - VOLUME 2**

_____ **GREAT _PEOPLE_ OF THE GREAT PLAINS - VOLUME 1**

at **$14.95 EACH** (plus $3.95 shipping & handling
for first book, add $2.00 for each additional book ordered.
Shipping and Handling costs for larger quantites available upon request.

Bill my: ❏ VISA   ❏ MasterCard   Expires _____

Card # _____

Signature _____

Daytime Phone Number _____

For credit card orders call 1-888-568-6329
TO ORDER ON-LINE VISIT: www.jmcompanies.com
OR SEND THIS ORDER FORM TO:
McCleery & Sons Publishing• PO Box 248 • Gwinner, ND 58040-0248
I am enclosing $_____   ❏ Check   ❏ Money Order
Payable in US funds. No cash accepted.

SHIP TO:
Name _____

Mailing Address _____

City _____

State/Zip _____

Orders by check allow longer delivery time. Money order and credit card orders will be shipped within 48 hours. This offer is subject to change without notice.

Call 1-888-568-6329
to order by credit card OR order
on-line at www.jmcompanies.com

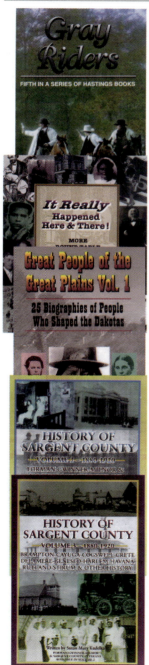

NEW RELEASES

Gray Riders
This is a flashback to Schanilec's Hastings Series mystery novels where Tom Hastings is the main character. Tom's great-grandfather, Thomas, lives on a farm with his family in western Missouri in 1861. The local citizenry react to the Union calvary by organizing and forming an armed group of horsemen who become known as the Gray Riders. The Riders not only defend their families and properties, but also ride with the Confederate Missouri Guard. They participate in three major battles. Written by Ernest Francis Schanilec. (266 pgs.) $16.95 each in a 6x9" paperback.

It Really Happened Here & There
This takes off where Ethelyn Pearson's "It Really Happened Here!" left off... More entertaining stories and true accounts: The Mystery of the Headless Hermit, Herman Haunts Sauk Centre, Hunting Trip Gone Wrong, The Swinging of Thomas Brown, Moltan Hell Created Creeping Molasses Disaster, Preachers Do Too!, Skinned Alive, Run Into A Blizzard or Burn!, Life and Death of Ol' Mother Feather Legs, How the Dakotans Fought Off Rustlers, and much more!!!! Written by Ethelyn Pearson - Author of *It Really Happened Here!*
(136 pages) $24.95 each in an 8-1/2 x 11" paperback.

Great People of the Great Plains Vol. 1
25 Biographies of People Who Shaped the Dakotas
This is the second book for Keith Norman and the first in this series. Keith has always had an interest in the history of the region. His radio show 'Great Stories of the Great Plains' is heard on great radio stations all across both Dakotas. For more information on the radio show and a list of his current affiliates check out Norman's website at www.tumbleweednetwork.com.
Written by Keith Norman - Author of *Great Stories of the Great Plains - Tales of the Dakotas* (124 pgs.)
$14.95 each in a 6x9" paperback.

History of Sargent County - Volume 2 - 1880-1920
(Forman, Gwinner, Milnor & Sargent County Veterans)
Over 220 photos and seven chapters containing: Forman, Gwinner and Milnor, North Dakota history with surveyed maps from 1909. Plus Early History of Sargent County, World War I Veterans, Civil War Veterans and Sargent County Fair History.
Written by: Susan Mary Kudelka - Author of *Early History of Sargent County - Volume 1* (224 pgs.)
$16.95 each in a 6x9" paperback.

History of Sargent County - Volume 3 - 1880-1920
(Brampton, Cayuga, Cogswell, Crete, DeLamere, Geneseo, Harlem, Havana, Rutland, Stirum & Other History)
Over 280 photos and fifteen chapters containing: Brampton, Cayuga, Cogswell, Crete, DeLamere, Geneseo, Harlem, Havana, Rutland and Stirum, North Dakota histories with surveyed maps from 1909. Plus history on Sargent County in WWI, Sargent County Newspapers, E. Hamilton Lee and bonus photo section.
Written by: Susan Mary Kudelka - Author of *Early History of Sargent County - Volume 1* (220 pgs.)
$16.95 each in a 6x9" paperback.

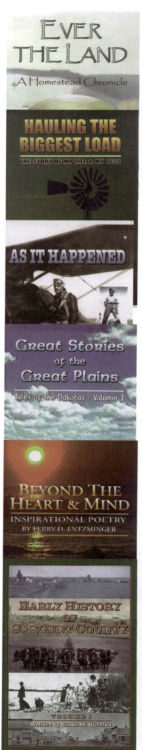

Ever The Land - *A Homestead Chronicle*
This historical chronicle (non-fiction) traces the life of young Pehr through his youth in the 1800's, marriage, parenthood and tenant farming in Sweden; then his emigration to America and homesteading in Minnesota. Multifarious simple joys and woes, and one deep constant sorrow accompany Pehr to his grave in 1914.
Written by: The late Ruben L. Parson (336 pgs.)
$16.96 each in a 6x9" paperback.

Hauling the Biggest Load - *The Story of My Life & My Loss*
This is an unusual story because of the many changes that have happened since the author's birth in 1926. In May 2002, he lost his son, John, in a car accident. None of those other experiences seemed important anymore... Richard needed something to try and take his mind off that tragedy. "I thought I had hauled some big loads in my life but I never had to have a load as big as this one."
Written by: Richard Hamann (144 pages)
$14.95 each in 6x9" paperback.

As It Happened
Over 40 photos and several chapters containing Allen Saunders' early years, tales of riding the rails, his Navy career, marriage, Army instruction, flying over "The Hump", and his return back to North Dakota. Written by Allen E. Saunders. (74 pgs)
$12.95 each in a 6x9" paperback.

Great Stories of the Great Plains - *Tales of the Dakotas - Vol. 1*
The radio show "Great Stories of the Great Plains" is heard on great radio stations all across both Dakotas. Norman has taken some of the stories from broadcasts, added some details, and even added some complete new tales to bring together this book of North and South Dakota history. Written by Keith Norman. (134 pgs.)
$14.95 each in a 6x9" paperback.

Beyond the Heart & Mind
Inspirational Poetry by Terry D. Entzminger
Beyond the Heart & Mind is the first in a series of inspirational poetry collections of Entzminger. Read and cherish over 100 original poems and true-to-the-heart verses printed in full color in the following sections: Words of Encouragement, On the Wings of Prayer, God Made You Very Special, Feelings From Within, The True Meaning of Love, and Daily Joys. (120 pgs.)
$12.95 each in a 6x9" paperback.

Early History of Sargent County - *Volume 1*
Over seventy photos and thirty-five chapters containing the early history of Sargent County, North Dakota: Glacial Movement in Sargent County, Native Americans in Sargent County, Weather, Memories of the Summer of 1883, Fight for the County Seat, Townships, Surveyed Maps from 1882 and much more.
Written by Susan M. Kudelka. (270 pgs.)
$16.95 each in a 6x9" paperback.

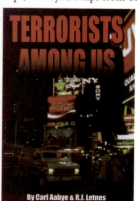

Terrorists Among Us
This piece of fiction was written to "expose a weakness" in present policies and conflicts in the masses of rules which seem to put emphasis on business, money, and power interests at the expense of the people's security, safety and happiness. Shouldn't we and our leaders strive for some security for our people? Written by Carl Aabye & R.J. Letnes. (178 pgs.)
$15.95 each in a 6x9" paperback.

THE HASTINGS SERIES

Blue Darkness *(First in a Series of Hastings Books)*
This tale of warm relationships and chilling murders takes place in the lake country of central Minnesota. Normal activities in the small town of New Dresen are disrupted when local resident, ex-CIA agent Maynard Cushing, is murdered. His killer, Robert Ranforth also an ex-CIA agent, had been living anonymously in the community for several years. Stalked and attached at his country home, Tom Hastings employs tools and people to mount a defense and help solve crimes. Written by Ernest Francis Schanilec (author of The Towers). (276 pgs.)
$16.95 each in a 6x9" paperback.

The Towers *(Second in a Series of Hastings Books)*
Tom Hastings has moved from the lake country of central Minnesota to Minneapolis. His move was precipitated by the trauma associated with the murder of one of his neighbors. After renting an apartment on the 20th floor of a high-rise apartment building known as The Towers, he's met new friends and retained his relationship with a close friend, Julie, from St. Paul. Hastings is a resident of the high-rise for less than a year when a young lady is found murdered next to a railroad track, a couple of blocks from The Towers. The murderer shares the same elevators, lower-level garage and other areas in the high-rise as does Hastings. The building manager and other residents, along with Hastings are caught up in dramatic events that build to a crisis while the local police are baffled. Who is the killer? Written by Ernest Francis Schanilec. (268 pgs.) $16.95 each in a 6x9" paperback.

Danger In The Keys *(Third in a Series of Hastings Books)*
Tom Hastings is looking forward to a month's vacation in Florida. While driving through Tennessee, he witnesses an automobile leaving the road and plunging down a steep slope. He stops and assists another man in finding the car. The driver, a young woman, survives the accident. Tom is totally unaware that the young woman was being chased because she had chanced coming into possession of a valuable gem, which had been heisted from a Saudi Arabian prince in a New York hotel room. After arriving in Key Marie Island in Florida, Tom checks in and begins enjoying the surf and the beach. He meets many interesting people, however, some of them are on the island because of the Guni gem, and they will stop at nothing in order to gain possession. Desperate people and their greedy ambitions interrupt Tom's goal of a peaceful vacation. Written by Ernest Francis Schanilec (210 pgs.)
$16.95 each in a 6x9" paperback.

Purgatory Curve *(Fourth in a Series of Hastings Books)*
A loud horn penetrated the silence on a September morning in New Dresden, Minnesota. Tom Hastings stepped onto the Main Street sidewalk after emerging from the corner Hardware Store. He heard a freight train coming and watched in horror as it crushed a pickup truck that was stalled on the railroad tracks. Moments before the crash, he saw someone jump from the cab. An elderly farmer's body was later recovered from the mangled vehicle. Tom was interviewed by the sheriff the next day and was upset that his story about what he saw wasn't believed. The tragic death of the farmer was surrounded with controversy and mysterious people, including a nephew who taunted Tom after the accident. Or, was it an accident?   Written by Ernest Francis Schanilec (210 pgs.) $16.95 each in a 6x9" paperback.

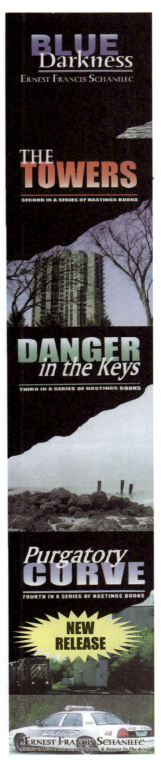

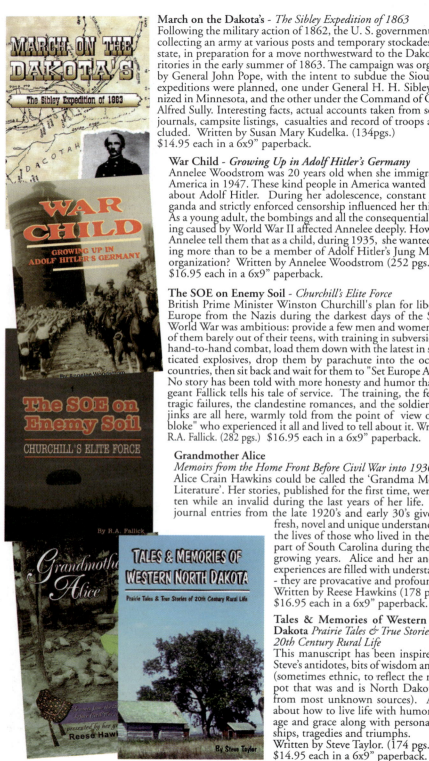

March on the Dakota's - *The Sibley Expedition of 1863*
Following the military action of 1862, the U. S. government began collecting an army at various posts and temporary stockades of the state, in preparation for a move northwestward to the Dakota Territories in the early summer of 1863. The campaign was organized by General John Pope, with the intent to subdue the Sioux. Two expeditions were planned, one under General H. H. Sibley, organized in Minnesota, and the other under the Command of General Alfred Sully. Interesting facts, actual accounts taken from soldiers' journals, campsite listings, casualties and record of troops also included. Written by Susan Mary Kudelka. (134pgs.) $14.95 each in a 6x9" paperback.

War Child - *Growing Up in Adolf Hitler's Germany*
Annelee Woodstrom was 20 years old when she immigrated to America in 1947. These kind people in America wanted to hear about Adolf Hitler. During her adolescence, constant propaganda and strictly enforced censorship influenced her thinking. As a young adult, the bombings and all the consequential suffering caused by World War II affected Annelee deeply. How could Annelee tell them that as a child, during 1935, she wanted nothing more than to be a member of Adolf Hitler's Jung Maidens' organization? Written by Annelee Woodstrom (252 pgs.) $16.95 each in a 6x9" paperback.

The SOE on Enemy Soil - *Churchill's Elite Force*
British Prime Minister Winston Churchill's plan for liberating Europe from the Nazis during the darkest days of the Second World War was ambitious: provide a few men and women, most of them barely out of their teens, with training in subversion and hand-to-hand combat, load them down with the latest in sophisticated explosives, drop them by parachute into the occupied countries, then sit back and wait for them to "Set Europe Ablaze." No story has been told with more honesty and humor than Sergeant Fallick tells his tale of service. The training, the fear, the tragic failures, the clandestine romances, and the soldiers' high jinks are all here, warmly told from the point of view of "one bloke" who experienced it all and lived to tell about it. Written by R.A. Fallick. (282 pgs.) $16.95 each in a 6x9" paperback.

Grandmother Alice
Memoirs from the Home Front Before Civil War into 1930's
Alice Crain Hawkins could be called the 'Grandma Moses of Literature'. Her stories, published for the first time, were written while an invalid during the last years of her life. These journal entries from the late 1920's and early 30's gives us a fresh, novel and unique understanding of the lives of those who lived in the upper part of South Carolina during the state's growing years. Alice and her ancestors experiences are filled with understanding - they are provacative and profound. Written by Reese Hawkins (178 pgs.) $16.95 each in a 6x9" paperback.

Tales & Memories of Western North Dakota *Prairie Tales & True Stories of 20th Century Rural Life*
This manuscript has been inspired with Steve's antidotes, bits of wisdom and jokes (sometimes ethnic, to reflect the melting pot that was and is North Dakota; and from most unknown sources). A story about how to live life with humor, courage and grace along with personal hardships, tragedies and triumphs.
Written by Steve Taylor. (174 pgs.) $14.95 each in a 6x9" paperback.

Phil Lempert's HEALTHY, WEALTHY, & WISE
The Shoppers Guide for Today's Supermarket
This is the must-have tool for getting the most for your money in every aisle. With this valuable advice you will never see (or shop) the supermarket the same way again. You will learn how to: save at least $1,000 a year on your groceries, guarantee satisfaction on every shopping trip, get the most out of coupons or rebates, avoid marketing gimmicks, create the ultimate shopping list, read and understand the new food labels, choose the best supermarkets for you and your family. Written by Phil Lempert. (198 pgs.)
$9.95 each in a 6x9" paperback.

Miracles of COURAGE
The Larry W. Marsh Story
This story is for anyone looking for simple formulas for overcoming insurmountable obstacles. At age 18, Larry lost both legs in a traffic accident and learned to walk again on untested prosthesis. No obstacle was too big for him - putting himself through college - to teaching a group of children that frustrated the whole educational system - to developing a nationally recognized educational program to help these children succeed. Written by Linda Marsh. (134 pgs.)
$12.95 each in a 6x9" paperback.

The Garlic Cure
Learn about natural breakthroughs to outwit: Allergies, Arthritis, Cancer, Candida Albicans, Colds, Flu and Sore Throat, Environmental and Body Toxins, Fatigue, High Cholesterol, High Blood Pressure and Homocysteine and Sinus Headaches. The most comprehensive, factual and brightly written health book on garlic of all times. INCLUDES: 139 GOURMET GARLIC RECIPES! Written by James F. Scheer, Lynn Allison and Charlie Fox. (240 pgs.)
$14.95 each in a 6x9" paperback.

I Took The Easy Way Out
Life Lessons on Hidden Handicaps
Twenty-five years ago, Tom Day was managing a growing business - holding his own on the golf course and tennis court. He was living in the fast lane. For the past 25 years, Tom has spent his days in a wheelchair with a spinal cord injury. Attendants serve his every need. What happened to Tom? We get an honest account of the choices Tom made in his life. It's a courageous story of reckoning, redemption and peace. Written by Thomas J. Day. (200 pgs.)
$19.95 each in a 6x9" paperback.

9/11 and Meditation - *America's Handbook*
All Americans have been deeply affected by the terrorist events of and following 9-11-01 in our country. David Thorson submits that meditation is a potentially powerful intervention to ameliorate the frightening effects of such divisive and devastating acts of terror. This book features a lifetime of harrowing life events amidst intense psychological and social polarization, calamity and chaos; overcome in part by practicing the age-old art of meditation. Written by David Thorson. (110 pgs.)
$9.95 each in a 4-1/8 x 7-1/4" paperback.

From Graystone to Tombstone
Memories of My Father Engolf Snortland 1908-1976
This haunting memoir will keep you riveted with true accounts of a brutal penitentiary to a manhunt in the unlikely little town of Tolna, North Dakota. At the same time the reader will emerge from the book with a towering respect for the author, a man who endured pain, grief and needless guilt -- but who learned the art of forgiving and writes in the spirit of hope. Written by Roger Snortland. (178 pgs.)
$16.95 each in a 6x9" paperback.

Blessed Are The Peacemakers *Civil War in the Ozarks*
A rousing tale that traces the heroic Rit Gatlin from his enlistment in the Confederate Army in Little Rock to his tragic loss of a leg in a Kentucky battle, to his return in the Ozarks. He becomes engaged in guerilla warfare with raiders who follow no flag but their own. Rit finds himself involved with a Cherokee warrior, slaves and romance in a land ravaged by war. Written by Joe W. Smith (444 pgs.)
$19.95 each in a 6 x 9 paperback

Pycnogenol®
Pycnogenol® for Superior Health presents exciting new evidence about nature's most powerful antioxidant. Pycnogenol® improves your total health, reduces risk of many diseases, safeguards your arteries, veins and entire circulation system. It protects your skin - giving it a healthier, smoother younger glow. Pycnogenol® also boosts your immune system. Read about it's many other beneficial effects. Written by Richard A. Passwater, Ph.D. (122 pgs.)
$5.95 each in a 4-1/8 x 6-7/8" paperback.

Remembering Louis L'Amour
Reese Hawkins was a close friend of Louis L'Amour, one of the fastest selling writers of all time. Now Hawkins shares this friendship with L'Amour's legion of fans. Sit with Reese in L'Amour's study where characters were born and stories came to life. Travel with Louis and Reese in the 16 photo pages in this memoir. Learn about L'Amour's lifelong quest for knowledge and his philosophy of life. Written by Reese Hawkins and his daughter Meredith Hawkins Wallin. (178 pgs.)
$16.95 each in a 5-1/2x8" paperback.

Outward Anxiety - Inner Calm
Steve Crociata is known to many as the Optician to the Stars. He was diagnosed with a baffling form of cancer. The author has processed experiences in ways which uniquely benefit today's readers. We learn valuable lessons on how to cope with distress, how to marvel at God, and how to win at the game of life. Written by Steve Crociata (334 pgs.)
$19.95 each in a 6 x 9 paperback

For Your Love
Janelle, a spoiled socialite, has beauty and breeding to attract any mate she desires. She falls for Jared, an accomplished man who has had many lovers, but no real love. Their hesitant romance follows Jared and Janelle across the ocean to exciting and wild locations. Join in a romance and adventure set in the mid-1800's in America's grand and proud Southland.
Written by Gunta Stegura. (358 pgs.)
$16.95 each in a 6x9" paperback.

Bonanza Belle
In 1908, Carrie Amundson left her home to become employed on a bonanza farm. Carrie married and moved to town. One tragedy after the other befell her and altered her life considerably and she found herself back on the farm where her family lived the toiled during the Great Depression. Carrie was witness to many life-changing events happenings. She changed from a carefree girl to a woman of great depth and stamina.
Written by Elaine Ulness Swenson. (344 pgs.)
$15.95 each in a 6x8-1/4" paperback.

Home Front
Read the continuing story of Carrie Amundson, whose life in North Dakota began in *Bonanza Belle*. This is the story of her family, faced with the challenges, sacrifices and hardships of World War II. Everything changed after the Pearl Harbor attack, and ordinary folk all across America, on the home front, pitched in to help in the war effort. Even years after the war's end, the effects of it are still evident in many of the men and women who were called to serve their country.
Written by Elaine Ulness Swenson. (304 pgs.)
$15.95 each in a 6x8-1/4" paperback.

First The Dream
This story spans ninety years of Anna's life - from Norway to America - to finding love and losing love. She and her family experience two world wars, flu epidemics, the Great Depression, droughts and other quirks of Mother Nature and the Vietnam War. A secret that Anna has kept is fully revealed at the end of her life. Written by Elaine Ulness Swenson. (326 pgs.)
$15.95 each in a 6x8-1/4" paperback

Pay Dirt
An absorbing story reveals how a man with the courage to follow his dream found both gold and unexpected adventure and adversity in Interior Alaska, while learning that human nature can be the most unpredictable of all.
Written by Otis Hahn & Alice Vollmar. (168 pgs.)
$15.95 each in a 6x9" paperback.

Spirits of Canyon Creek *Sequel to "Pay Dirt"*
Hahn has a rich stash of true stories about his gold mining experiences. This is a continued successful collaboration of battles on floodwaters, facing bears and the discovery of gold in the Yukon. Written by Otis Hahn & Alice Vollmar. (138 pgs.)
$15.95 each in a 6x9" paperback.

Seasons With Our Lord
Original seasonal and special event poems written from the heart. Feel the mood with the tranquil color photos facing each poem. A great coffee table book or gift idea. Written by Cheryl Lebahn Hegvik. (68 pgs.)
$24.95 each in a 11x8-1/2 paperback.

Damsel in a Dress
Escape into a world of reflection and after thought with this second printing of Larson's first poetry book. It is her intention to connect people with feelings and touch the souls of people who have experienced similiar times. Lynne emphasizes the belief that everything happens for a reason. After all, with every event in life come lessons...we grow from hardships. It gives us character and it made her who she is. Written by Lynne D. Richard Larson (author of Eat, Drink & Remarry) (86 pgs.) $12.95 each in a 5x8" paperback.

Eat, Drink & Remarry
The poetry in this book is taken from different experiences in Lynne's life and from different geographical and different emotional places. Every poem is an inspiration from someone or a direct event from their life...or from hers. Every victory and every mistake - young or old. They slowly shape and mold you into the unique person you are. Celebrate them as rough times that you were strong enough to endure. Written by Lynne D. Richard Larson (86 pgs.) $12.95 each in a 5x8" paperback.

Country-fied
Stories with a sense of humor and love for country and small town people who, like the author, grew up country-fied . . . Country-fied people grow up with a unique awareness of their dependence on the land. They live their lives with dignity, hard work, determination and the ability to laugh at themselves. Written by Elaine Babcock. (184 pgs.) $14.95 each in a 6x9" paperback.

Charlie's Gold and Other Frontier Tales
Kamron's first collection of short stories gives you adventure tales about men and women of the west, made up of cowboys, Indians, and settlers. Written by Kent Kamron. (174 pgs.) $15.95 each in a 6x9" paperback.

A Time For Justice
This second collection of Kamron's short stories takes off where the first volume left off, satisfying the reader's hunger for more tales of the wide prairie. Written by Kent Kamron. (182 pgs.) $16.95 each in a 6x9" paperback.

It Really Happened Here!
Relive the days of farm-to-farm salesmen and hucksters, of ghost ships and locust plagues when you read Ethelyn Pearson's collection of strange but true tales. It captures the spirit of our ancestors in short, easy to read, colorful accounts that will have you yearning for more. Written by Ethelyn Pearson. (168 pgs.) $24.95 each in an 8-1/2x11" paperback.

The Silk Robe
- Dedicated to Shari Lynn Hunt, a wonderful woman who passed away from cancer. Mom lived her life with unfailing faith, an open loving heart and a giving spirit. She is remembered for her compassion and gentle strength. Written by Shaunna Privratsky. $6.95 each in a 4-1/4x5-1/2" booklet. *Complimentary notecard and envelope included.*

(Add $3.95 shipping & handling for first book, add $2.00 for each additional book ordered.)